The Shape Changer

# The Shape Changer

## Keith Laumer

A BERKLEY MEDALLION BOOK
PUBLISHED BY
BERKLEY PUBLISHING CORPORATION

This book is dedicated to my brother, Frank.

LIBRARY OF CONGRESS CATALOG CARD NUMBER:
71-171473

SBN 425-02363-X

BERKLEY MEDALLION BOOKS *are published by*
*Berkley Publishing Corporation*
*200 Madison Avenue*
*New York, N.Y. 10016*

BERKLEY MEDALLION BOOKS ® TM 757,375

Printed in the United States of America

Berkley Medallion Edition, JUNE, 1973

# CHAPTER ONE

## 1

The moon shone bright on the palace gardens as Sir Lafayette O'Leary stepped stealthily forth from the scullery entrance. Silently, he tiptoed along the graveled path which led beneath a rhododendron hedge, skirting the royal Artesian vegetable garden and winding past the chicken yard, where a sleepy hen clucked irritably at his passing. At the street gate he paused to glance back at the dark towers looming against the cloud-bright sky. A faint light shone behind the windows on his third floor apartment. Up there Daphne was curled between silken sheets, waiting for him. He had sent her off to bed alone, telling her he'd join her as soon as he'd perused another chapter of his newest book on Mesmeric Science; instead, here he was, creeping out like a thief in the night, on his way to a stealthy rendezvous with a person or persons unknown—all because of that ridiculous note he'd found tucked under the napkin accompanying his after-dinner drink.

He pulled the grubby scrap of paper from his pocket, reread it by the dim glow from a lamp in a bracket on the wall.

"Deer Sir Laffeyet,
I doant sea you in kwite a wile, but you bin on my mind
plenty. The reezin I rite you this letter is, I got holt of a
item witch its two big to handle aloan. I cant sa no
more now, wich some fink mite get holt of it and steel a
march on us. But meat me at midnite at Ye Ax and
Draggin, an I will fill you in.
X (his mark)"

"It must be from the Red Bull," Lafayette told himself.
"Nobody else could spell as creatively as this. But why the
cloak-and-poniard approach? You'd think he was still cutting purses for a living, instead of being a lionized hero
with the royal pardon and the Order of the Dragon for his
services to the crown. Which suggests that he's up to his
old tricks. It's probably some wild scheme for counter-
feiting quarters, or turning base metal into gold. If I had
good sense, I'd turn around right now and forget the whole
thing. . . ."

But instead of turning back, he thrust the note into his
pocket and let himself out the gate. Here in the narrow
side street, the wind seemed chiller, bearing with it a whiff
from the palace sty, where a pair of prize China pigs
awaited the next feast day. Lafayette heard a mournful
snort as he passed. In the far corner of the enclosure,
George, the four-hundred-pound boar, huddled against the
wall, as if recoiling from the advances of the scarcely less
bulky Jemimah.

"Poor George," Lafayette murmured. "Maybe you've
been cursed with too much imagination—like me."

At that moment, George seemed to catch his eye. With
a frantic lunge he eluded the amorous sow, scrambled
toward Lafayette, making piteous gobbling sounds.

"Don't make the same mistake I do, George, of not ap-
preciating what you've got while you've got it," Lafayette
advised the giant hog as it attempted unsuccessfully to rear
up against the fence only to fall back with a loud *squelch!*
into the mud.

"Go to Jemimah, tell her you're sorry, and forget the inevitable barbecue—" Lafayette broke off as George hurled himself at the fence, eliciting an ominous creak from the stout boards.

"Shhh!" he hissed. "You'll rouse the palace guards! Be sensible, George. Gather ye rosebuds while ye may . . ." But as he hurried off along the dark street, the mournful sounds followed him.

Few of the leaded glass windows set in the half-timbered gables overhanging the cobbled street showed lights; the honest folk of the capital were abed at this hour. Only dubious characters like himself—and the man he was going to meet—were abroad now, Lafayette reflected guiltily. In the distance he heard the *haloo* of a city watchman making his rounds, the barking of a dog, the tinkle of a bell. A steam-carriage rumbled past the intersection ahead, a red lantern swaying at its tailgate, its iron-shod wheels groaning against the paving blocks. Beyond, he saw a sign board bearing a familiar device: the prow of a Viking ship and a two-handled battle-ax. Below it was a low, wide, oaken door, iron bound, with heavy strap hinges. The sight brought back piquant memories. The Ax and Dragon had been the scene of his arrival in Artesia some years before—transported instantaneously from Colby Corners, USA, by the Psychic Energies focused by the Hypnotic Art, as described by Professor Doktor Hans Joseph Schimmerkopf in his massive volume on Mesmeric Science. It had also been the scene of his immediate arrest by the King's musketeers on a charge of sorcery, brought about by his careless decanting of several gallons of vintage wine from a one-liter bottle. He had managed to quash the indictment only by the desperate expedient of promising to slay a dragon. Well, in the end he had slain the dragon—one of them. The other had become his pet and favorite steed. He had also eliminated the fearsome two-headed giant Lod, which was rather a shame in a way; one of the heads hadn't been a bad sort of chap at all. Lafayette had gone on to depose the usurper, Goruble, and restore the throne to Princess Adoranne. Ever since, he—and his charming former chambermaid, Daphne—had been honored citizens of the quaint kingdom of Artesia, occupying a spacious apartment in the West Palace Annex, and on the closest terms with Adoranne and Prince Alain, her consort.

And now, here he was, back out in the cold, dark street, again approaching the door that had led him to such adventures, so long ago.

But there'd be no adventures this time, he told himself sternly. He had learned his lesson the last time he had found himself feeling impatient with the peaceful life. His meddling had gotten him involved on a mad assignment from Central—the head office of the Inter-dimensional Monitor Service—which had almost left him stranded in a deserted parallel world. No, this time he would know better. He had just come as a lark, actually. In a way it was rather jolly shivering in the cold, remembering his early days as a penniless draftsman, holed up in Mrs. McGlint's Clean Rooms and Board, subsisting on sardines and daydreams—but only because he had a cozy bed waiting for him back in the palace. Wouldn't it be ghastly, he thought, to *really* be some homeless gypsy, out on the tiles at this hour, chilled to the bone and hungry, with no relief in sight?

"That's enough gloomy thinking," he told himself firmly as he reached the tavern door. "In an hour I'll be snuggled up with Daphne, all the better for a brisk stroll in the night air." He adjusted a look of amused complacency on his face, shook out his cloak, and stepped into the warmth and beery aroma of the Ax and Dragon.

A bed of coals glowing in the ox-sized fireplace dimly illuminated the long, low room, the plank tables ranked along one side, the wine and ale kegs along the other. But for the silent bartender behind the trestle bar, the place seemed deserted, until a large figure rose among the shadows at the rear.

"Over dis way, bub!" a hearty voice growled. "Take a load off duh dogs, an' we'll hoist a few in membry o' duh old days!"

"Red Bull!" Lafayette exclaimed, ducking his head under the low, age-blackened beams. "I thought it would be you!" He clasped the calloused hand of the big man who beamed at him, his little red-rimmed eyes agleam in his lumped, scarred face. There was a little gray now, Lafayette noticed, in the bristly red thatch above the cauliflowered ears. Otherwise the soft life hadn't changed the former outlaw.

"Where've you been keeping yourself?" Lafayette demanded as he took the proferred chair. "I haven't seen you in a year or more."

"Take a tip from a pal," the Red Bull said sadly as he poured wine into O'Leary's glass. "Stay away from dem hick jails."

"You haven't been up to your old tricks?" Lafayette demanded in a severe tone. "I thought you'd reformed, Red Bull."

"Naw—dey nabs me on account of I was astride a nag which it had some udder mug's brand on. But, geeze, youse know how all dese bay mares look alike on duh parking lot."

"I warned you about your casual view of property rights," Lafayette said. "The first night we met—right here at this very table."

"Yeah—I picked duh spot fer duh sentimental associations," the big man acknowledged. He sighed. "Youse had duh right idear, chum: youse give up duh cutpurse racket and went straight, and now—"

"Are you back on that old idea?" Lafayette said sharply. "I was never a cutpurse. I don't know how you got that impression—"

"Dat's right, pal, don't admit nothing." The Red Bull winked, a grotesque twisting of battered features. "It'll be our little secret dat youse used to be duh Phantom Highwayman, duh dread specter o' duh moors."

"That's a lot of rubbish, Red Bull," Lafayette said, sampling his wine. "Just because the first time you saw me I was wearing a coat of claret velvet and breeches of brown doeskin—"

"Yeah, an' dey fitted wit' never a wrinkle, right? An' dey come up to your thigh. An' yuh had a French cocked hat on your forehead, and a bunch of lace at your chin—"

"That doesn't mean a thing! It just happened to be what I conjured up—I mean," he corrected, seeing that he was about to complicate matters: the Red Bull would never understand the Focusing of the Psychical Energies. "I mean, I actually intended to wear a gray suit and a Homburg, but something went a little awry, and—"

"Sure, sure, I heard all dat sweet jazz before, pal. Anyways, I seen by duh papers dis would be a night when duh moon would be like a ghostly galleon, and duh wind would be a torrent o' darkness, an' all, so I sez—"

"Will you come to the point?" Lafayette snapped. "It's actually long after my bedtime, and—"

"Sure chum. Drink your wine whilst I fill youse in. It's like dis, see? I'm ankling along duh pike, on my way back from duh burg where dey hung duh frame on me, an' I'm overtook by nightfall. So I seeks shelter in a cave an' in duh morning what was my surprise to find duh rock I was using fer a piller was ackshully a neat little cask like, you know, a safety deposit box."

"Oh?"

"Yeah. So, I'm shaking it around a little, and duh lids falls open. And guess what's inside?"

"Money? Jewels?" Lafayette hazarded, swallowing more wine. It was poor stuff, thin and sour. Too bad Central was keeping that Supressor focused on him; otherwise they could have just as easily been drinking Château Lafite-Rothschild. . . .

"Naw," the Red Bull said disgustedly. "Dere was just some kind o' gadget, like a combination can opener and hot-patch kit. Only it looks like it's broke. I'm about to t'row it away, when I notice duh lettering on duh bottom."

"What did it say?" Lafayette inquired, yawning. " 'Made in Japan'?"

"Take a look fer yourself, pal." The Red Bull dipped a set of scarred knuckles inside his grimy leather jerkin, withdrew a small apparatus of the approximate appearance of a six-inch-high patent coffee maker—or possibly a miniature jukebox, Lafayette corrected himself. There was a round base, painted a dark red, surmounted by a clear plastic box inside which were visible a maze of wires, wheels, levers, gears, tiny bits of colored glass and plastic.

"What in the world is it?" he inquired. "Why, those look like condensers and transistors—but that's silly. No one's invented transistors yet, in Artesia."

"Great, chum!" the Red Bull exclaimed. "I knowed youse would have duh straight dope!"

"I don't have any dope, straight or otherwise," O'Leary objected. "I haven't the faintest idea what the thing is." He turned it around, frowning at it. "What does it do, Red Bull?"

"Huh? Beats me, bub. But what I figger is, it's gotta do *some*thing nifty—and all we got to do is dope out what, and we're in business!"

"Nonsense." Lafayette pushed the apparatus away. "Red Bull, it was nice seeing you again, but I'm afraid you're wasting my time with this Rube Goldberg. Are you sure you didn't cobble it up yourself? I never saw mechanical and electronic components jumbled together like that—"

11

"Whom, I?" The Red Bull said indignantly. "Pal, I wouldn't string youse! Like I says, I find duh gimcrack in duh cave, an'—"

"Phooey, Red Bull." Lafayette finished his wine and pushed the mug back. "I'm going home and to bed, where I belong. Drop around some evening and we'll talk over the good old days when I was a poor, homeless boob, with no friends, no money, and a death sentence hanging over me."

"Hey, wait, pal! You ain't seen what's wrote on duh buttom, which I din't t'row it away when I seen it!"

Lafayette grunted impatiently, picked up the gadget and peered at the underside of the base. He frowned, held it in a better light.

"Well," he exclaimed. "Why didn't you say so? This could be something important. Where did you say you found it?"

"Buried in duh cave. And as soon as I seen duh royal coat of arms, I glommed I was onto something big, right, pal?"

"Goruble's personal cartouche," Lafayette muttered. "But it looks as if it were stamped in the metal with a hand-punch. There's something else . . ."

"What does it say, chum?" The Red Bull leaned forward eagerly.

"Haven't you read it?" Lafayette inquired in surprise.

"Uh—I din't go in much fer duh scholar bit when I was a nipper," the big man said abashedly.

"It's difficult to read in this light—but I can make out . . . PROPERTY OF CENTRAL PROBABILITY LABORATORY." He rubbed a finger at the tarnished surface; more letters appeared:

FOCAL REFERENT—VARIABLE (FULL RANGE) MARK III

WARNING—EXPERIMENTAL MODEL

FOR USE BY AUTHORIZED PERSONNEL ONLY

"Chee," the Red Bull said reverently.

"Why, good lord," Lafayette said, "I'll bet this is part of the loot Goruble brought along to Artesia when he defected from the Central Monitor Service, twenty-five years ago! I remember that Nicodaeus said they'd recovered a Traveler-load of stuff from the lab he'd rigged up in the palace catacombs, but that the records seemed to indicate there was more that they couldn't find—" He broke off. "Red Bull—that cave—could you find it again? There might be a whole trove of other items there!"

"Dat's what I been tryna tell youse, pal," the former second-story man said aggrievedly. "Oncet I seen I was onto duh real goods, I dig around and come up wit' a whole bunch o' wild-looking gear under duh floor! I can't carry all duh stuff, so I bury it again, and come hot-footing to youse wit' duh whole story."

"Ye gods, Red Bull—this stuff is dynamite! If it fell into the wrong hands—"

"Right, bub! Dat's why I think of youse! Now, duh way I got duh caper doped, I bring in duh stuff a couple choice items at a time, see, and wit' your old contacts from when youse was in duh game, we could soon retire on duh take!"

"Take! Are you out of your mind? This stuff is experimental equipment from a temporal laboratory—where they run experiments in probability, time travel, interdimensional relationships! Start messing with this, and heaven only knows what kind of probability stresses you'd set up! You might shift half of Artesia into some other phase of existence—or even worse!"

The Red Bull was frowning darkly. "What's duh proposition got to do wit' timetables? And you can skip duh cracks about my relationships. I been keeping company wit' duh same frail for five years now, and all we ever do—"

"You don't understand, Red Bull! We can't sell this stuff! It belongs to Central! Goruble stole it! We have to get it back to them at once, before something terrible happens!"

"Listen, pal," the Red Bull said earnestly. "Duh worst t'ing I can see happening is fer some udder slob to latch onto duh gravy, see?"

"Red Bull, try to fix this thought in your mind," Lafayette said tautly. "The thing is potentially more dangerous than an atom bomb—not that you know what an atom bomb is. Just take my word for it that I have to turn it over to the Central authorities at once—if I can get hold of the authorities," he added doubtfully.

"Nix, pal." The Red Bull's immense hand closed around the device resting on the scarred table. "Turn duh goods over to duh bulls, and dey pocket duh spoils fer demselfs. Nuts to dat. If youse don't want a slice o' duh action, I'll work duh play solo!"

"No, Red Bull, you still don't get it! Listen—I promise you there'll be a fat reward for turning this in. Say—a hundred gold pieces."

"What about duh rest o' duh trove?" the Red Bull inquired suspiciously, rubbing a calloused hand across his stubbled chin with a sound like frying fat.

"We can't touch it. I'll use the special phone in Nicodaeus' old lab to put a call through to Central, and get an Inspector of Continua in here to take charge—"

"Youse was saying about duh reward. What say to ten grand, cash on duh line?"

"I'm sure it can be arranged. What about it, Red Bull? I'll see that your interests are protected."

"Well—it ain't like duh old days, bub. I still think youse and me would of been a great team, wit' my brains an' your neat tricks, like riding t'rough duh sky an' turning to smoke under duh very noses o' duh Johns—"

"You're talking nonsense, Red Bull. Just trust me: I'll see to it you don't lose by it. Now tell me—where is this cave, exactly?"

"Well . . . I dunno, pal," the Red Bull said doubtfully. "Youse are a square mug, an' all, but dis is duh biggest career opportunity dat ever come my way." He rose. "I got to go to duh can," he confided. "Grimme a minute to consider duh angles." He swaggered off toward the rear of the tavern. Lafayette picked up the Focal Referent, Mark III, and stared into the complexities of its interior. It resembled no machine he had ever seen before; it was as though the components of an eight-day clock and a portable TV had been mixed thoroughly and packed into the same restricted space. There was a small, flat button on one side, near the bottom, glowing with a faint, enticing glow. Lafayette poked at it. . . .

*The Universe turned inside out. Lafayette—clinging to the interior of the vast solid that surrounded the hollow bubble that was the earth—was dimly aware that his body now filled a void of infinite extent, while his eyes, situated at the exact center of reality, stared directly into each other, probing a bottomless nothingness that whirled, expanded, and—*

The walls of the room were sailing past, like a merry-go-round running down. Lafayette blinked dizzily, grabbed for his wine glass, took a hearty gulp, sat trembling and drawing deep, restorative breaths. He swallowed a lump the approximate size of a hard-boiled egg, edging as far as possible away from the innocent-looking apparatus sitting on the table before him.

"Oh, you're a genius, O'Leary," he muttered to himself, patting his pocket for a handkerchief with which to mop the cold sweat from his brow. "You give the Red Bull a lecture on the danger of meddling with experimental temporal lab equipment, and then you poke a button yourself, and nearly . . . nearly . . . do whatever I nearly did!"

There was a sudden sound of scuffling, emanating from the direction of the alley behind the tavern. The tapman came around the bar with a stout cudgel in his hand. He halted abruptly, staring at Lafayette.

"We're closed, you," he said roughly. "How'd ye get in here, anyway?"

"Through the door, Tom, as usual," Lafayette snapped. "What about it?"

"Haul ye'r freight, ye scurvy knave." The barman hooked a thick thumb over his shoulder. "Out!"

"What's got into you, Tom?" O'Leary said testily. "Go polish a glass or something—"

"Look, crum-bum—so I open the joint so me old mate the Red Bull could have a quiet rondy-vooz with a

15

nobleman; that don't mean every varlet on the pavement gets to warm hisself at me fire—"

"Some fire," Lafayette snapped. "The A & D used to be a fairly nice dive, as dives go—but I can see it's deteriorated—" He broke off with an *oof!* as Tom rammed the club into his short ribs, grasped him by the back of the neck, and assisted him from the bench.

"I says out, rogue, and out is what I mean!"

As the landlord sent him staggering toward the door, Lafayette caught at one of the posts supporting the sagging beams, whirled around it, and drove a straight right punch to the barman's chin, sending him bounding backward to end up on the packed-earth floor with his head under a table.

"I was just leaving, thanks," Lafayette said, noting as he seized the Mark III from the table that his voice had developed a hoarse, croaking sound. But no wonder, after the scare he'd had, followed by the unexpected attack by an old acquaintance. "I think you'd better lay off sampling the stock, Tom. It does nothing for your personality." He paused at the door to straighten his coat, smooth his lapels. The cloth felt unaccountably greasy. He looked down, stared aghast at grimy breeches, torn stockings, and run-over shoes.

"All that from one little scuffle?" he wondered aloud. The landlord was crawling painfully forth from under the table.

"Stick around, mister," he said blurrily. "It's two falls out o' three, remember?" As he came to his feet with a lurch, Lafayette slipped out into the dark street. A chill drizzle of rain had started up, driven by the gusty wind. The Red Bull was nowhere in sight.

"Now, where's he gotton to?" Lafayette wondered aloud as he reached to draw his cloak about him, only to discover that the warm garment was gone.

"Drat!" he said, turning back to the tavern door.

"Tom! I forgot something!" he shouted; but even as he spoke, the light faded inside. He rattled and pounded in vain. The oak panel was locked tight.

"Oh, perfect," he groaned aloud. "Now he's mad at me—and it was my second-best cloak, too, the one Daphne's Aunt Lardie made for me." He turned up his jacket collar—of stiff, coarse wool, he noted absently; funny, he'd grabbed a coat from the closet in the dark, but he didn't remember owning anything *this* disreputable. Maybe it belonged to the man who had come to clear the swallows' nest out of the chimney . . .

"But never mind that," he reminded himself firmly. "Getting this infernal machine into safe hands is the important thing. I'll lock it in the palace vault, and then try to get in touch with Central, and . . ." His train of thought was interrupted by the clank of heavy boots on the pavement of an alley which debouched from between narrow buildings a few yards ahead. O'Leary shied, reaching instinctively for his sword-hilt—

But of course he wasn't wearing a sword, he realized as his fingers closed on nothing. Hadn't worn one in years, except on gala occasions, and then just a light, bejeweled model that was strictly for show. But then, he hadn't been out in the midnight streets alone for quite a while. And it had never occurred to him tonight to do anything as melodramatic as buckling on the worn blade he'd used in the old days. . . .

As he hastily tucked the Mark III away out of sight, three men emerged from the alley mouth, all in floppy feathered hats, green-and-yellow-striped jackets— Adoranne's colors—wide scarlet sashes, baggy pants above carelessly rolled boots: The Royal City Guard.

"Oh, boy, am I glad to see you fellows," Lafayette greeted the trio. "I thought you were footpads or worse. Look, I need an escort back to the palace, and—"

"Stay, rogue!" the leading musketeer barked. "Up against the wall!"

"Turn around and put your hands against it, over your head, you know the routine!" a second guardsman commanded, hand on épé hilt.

"This is no time for jokes," O'Leary announced in some asperity. "I've got some hot cargo for the royal

17

vault—high-priority stuff. Shorty—" he addressed the smallest of the trio, a plump sergeant with fiercely curled mustachios,—"you lead the way, and you other two chaps fall in behind—"

"Don't go calling me by my nickname!" the short cop roared, whipping out his blade. "And we ain't no chaps!"

"What's got into you, Shorty?" Lafayette demanded in astonishment. "You're not mad just because I won two-fifty from you playing at skittles the other night—"

The sword leaped to prick his throat. "Jest you button the lip, Clyde, 'fore I pin you to the wall!" Shorty motioned curtly. "You boys frisk him. I got a funny feeling this bozo's here's more'n a routine vagrant."

"Are you all out of your minds?" O'Leary yelled as the guardsmen flung him roughly against the wall, began patting his pockets none too gently. "Shorty, do you really mean you don't recognize me?"

"Hey—hold it, boys," Shorty said. "Uh—turn around, you," he addressed Lafayette in an more uncertain tone. "You claim I know you, hah?" He frowned at him searchingly. "Well, maybe you went downhill since I seen you last . . . but I wouldn't want to turn my back on an old pal. What was the name again?"

"O'Leary!" Lafayette yelled. "Lafayette O'Leary *Sir* Lafayette O'Leary, if you want to get technical!"

"OK," Shorty rasped with a return to his gravelly voice. "You picked the wrong pigeon, stoop! It just so happens that me and Sir Lafayette are just like that!" He held up two fingers, close together, to indicate the intimacy of the relationship. "Why, on his first night in town, five years ago, Sir Lafayette done me a favor which I'll never forget it—me and Gertrude neither!"

"Right!" Lafayette cried. "That was just before I went all wavery and almost disappeared back to Mrs. McGlint's—and as a favor to your boys, I stuck around, just so you wouldn't have anything inexplicable to explain to the desk sergeant, right?"

"Hey," one of the troopers said. "Lookit what I found,

18

Sarge!" He held up a fat gold watch, shaped like a yellow turnip.

"W-where did that come from?" Lafayette faltered.

"And how about this?" A second man produced a jeweled pendant from O'Leary's other pocket. "And this!" He displayed a silver inlaid Elk's tooth, an ornate snuff-box with a diamond-studded crest, a fistful of lesser baubles. "Looks like your old pal has been working, Sarge!"

"I've been framed!" Lafayette cried. "Somebody planted that stuff on me!"

"That cuts it," the NCO snarled. "Try to make a monkey out o' me, will you? You'll be on magotty bread and green water for thirty days before your trial even comes up, wittold!"

"Let's just go back to the palace," Lafayette shouted. "We'll ask Daphne—Countess Daphne, to you, you moron—she'll confirm what I say! And after this is straightened out—"

"Put the cuffs on him, Fred," Shorty said. "Hubba hubba. We go off duty in ten minutes."

"Oh, no," Lafayette said, half to himself. "This isn't going to turn into one of those idiotic farces where everything goes from bad to worse just because no one has sense enough to explain matters. All I have to do is just speak calmly and firmly to these perfectly reasonable officers of the law, and—"

From the nearby alley there was a sudden rasp of shoe leather on cobbles. Shorty whirled, grabbing for his sword-hilt as dark figures loomed. There was a dull *thunk!* as of a ball bat striking a saddle; the stubby sergeant's feathered hat fell off, as its owner stumbled backward and went down. Even as their blades cleared their scabbards the other three musketeers received matching blows to the skull. They collapsed in a flutter of plumes, a flapping of silk, a clatter of steel. Three tall, dark men in the jeweled leathers and gaudy silks of a Wayfarers Tribe closed in about Lafayette.

"Let's get going, Zorro," one of them whispered in a

19

voice that was obviously the product of damaged vocal chords, substantiating the testimony of the welted scar across his brown throat, only partially concealed by a greasy scarf knotted there. A second member of the band—a one-eyed villian with a massive gold earring—was swiftly going through the pockets of the felled policemen.

"Hey—wait just a minute," O'Leary blurted, in confusion. "What's going on here? Who are you? Why did you slug the cops? What—"

"Losing your greep, Zorro?" the leader cut him off brusquely. "You could have knocked me over weeth a feether wheen I see you in the clutches of the *Roumi* dogs." He stooped, with a quick slash of a foot-long knife freed a dagger in an ornately worked sheath from the belt of the nearest musketeer. "Queek, compadres," he rasped. "Someone's coming theese way." He caught O'Leary's arm, began hauling him toward the alley mouth from which the raiders had pounced.

"Hold on, fellows!" Lafayette protested. "Look, I appreciate the gesture and all that, but it isn't necessary. I'll just turn myself in and make a clean breast of it, explain that it was all a general misunderstanding, and—"

"Poor Zorro, a blow on the head has meexed up his weets, Luppo," a short, swarthy man with a full beard grunted.

"Don't you understand?" Lafayette yelped sharply as he was hustled along the alley. "I *want* to go to court! You're just making it worse! And stop calling me Zorro! My name's O'Leary!"

The leader of the band swung Lafayette around to glare down into his face from a height of close to seven feet of leather, bone and muscle. "Worse? What does theese mean, Zorro? That you deedn't come through on your beeg brag, eh?" He gave O'Leary a bone-rattling shake. "And so you theenk instead of facing up to King Shosto, you'll do a leetle time in the *Roumi* breeg, ees that eet?"

"No, you big ape!" Lafayette yelled, and landed a solid kick to the bulky Wayfarer's shin. As the victim yelled and

20

bent to massage the injury, Lafayette jerked free, whirled—and was facing half a dozen bowie knives gripped in as many large, brown fists.

"Look, fellows, let's talk it over," Lafayette started. At that moment, there was a yell from the street where they had left the three musketeers. Lafayette opened his mouth to respond, caught only a glimpse of a cloak as it whirled at his head; then he was muffled in its sour-smelling folds, lifted from his feet, slung over a bony shoulder, and carried, jolting, from the scene.

# CHAPTER TWO

## 1

Bundled in the reeking cloak and trussed with ropes, Lafayette lay in what he deducted to be the bed of a wagon, judging from the sounds and odors of the horse, rumble of unshod wheels on cobbles, and the creak of harness. His attempts to shout for air had netted him painful blows, after which he had subsided and concentrated his efforts on avoiding suffocation. Now he lay quietly, his bruises throbbing with every jolt of the cumbersome vehicle.

At length the sound of cobbles gave way to the softer texture of an unpaved surface. Leather groaned as the wagon bed took on a tilt that testified to the ascent of a grade. The air grew cooler. At last, with a final lurch, all motion ceased. Lafayette struggled to sit up, was promptly seized and pitched over the side where waiting hands caught him, amid a gutteral exchange of questions and answers in a staccato dialect. The ropes were stripped away, then the muffling cloak. Lafayette sneezed, spat dust from his mouth, dug grit from his eyes and ears, and took a hearty breath of cool, resin-scented air.

He was standing in a clearing in the forest. Bright moonlight dazzled down through the high boughs of lofty pines on patched tents and high-wheeled wagons with once-garish paint jobs now faded to chipped and peeling pastel tones. A motley crowd of black-haired, olive-skinned men, women, and children, all dressed in soiled garments of bright, mismatched colors, stared solemnly at him. From tent flaps and the dim-lit windows of wagons more curious faces gazed. Except for the soft sigh of wind through the trees and the clop of a swaybacked horse shifting his hooves, the silence was total.

"Well," Lafayette began, but a spasm of coughing detracted from the tone of indignation. "I suppose (cough) you've kidnapped me (cough-cough) for a reason. . . ."

"Steeck around, Zorro. Don't get impatient," the one-eyed man said. "You'll geet the message queeck enough."

There was a stir in the ranks; the crowd parted.

An elderly man, still powerful-looking in spite of his grizzled hair and weather-beaten face, came forward. He was dressed in a purple satin shirt with pink armbands baggy chartreuse pants above short red boots with curled toes. There were rings on each of his thick fingers; a string of beads hung around his corded neck. Through his wide green alligator belt were thrust a bulky pistol and a big-bladed knife with glass emeralds and rubies set in the plastic handle. He planted himself before Lafayette, looking him up and down with an expression of sour disapproval on his not-recently-shaved mahogany-dark face.

"Ha!" he said. "So Meester Beeg-mouth Zorro, he not so hot like he theenk, hey?" He grasped a long hair curling from his nose, yanked it out, held it up, looking at it, let his narrowed eyes slide past it to Lafayette.

"Look, I don't know what this Zorro business is," O'Leary said, "but if you're in charge of this menagerie, how about detailing someone to take me back to town before matters get entirely out of hand? I can square things by saying a word to a chap in the records department and have the whole thing scratched off the blotter, and—"

"Ha!" the oldster cut Lafayette's speech short. "You theenk you weegle out of the seetuation by preteending you got bats een the belfry! But eet's no use, Zorro!

Theese is not the way the ancient Law of the Tribe, she works!"

A mutter of agreement rose from the bystanders. There were a few snickers; a single muffled sob came from a dark-eyed young creature in the front rank.

"What's your tribal law got to do with me?" Lafayette said hotly. "I was going quietly about my business when your gang of thugs grabbed me—"

"OK, I streeng along weeth the gang," the fierce-eyed old man interrupted with an ominous grin. "Last night, you dreenk a few bottles of Old Sulphuric, and you geet beeg ideas: you have the nerve to make a pass at the niece of the King! By the rule of the Tribe, theese offer, she cannot be ignored—even from a seemple-minded nobody like you! So—poor old King Shosto—he geeves you your chance!" The swarthy man smote himself on the chest.

"Look, you've got me mixed up with somebody else," Lafayette said. "My name is O'Leary, and—"

"But naturally, before you can have the preevilege of wooing Gizelle, you got to breeng home a trophy to qualify. For theese reason, you sleep eento the ceety under cover of darkness. I seend Luppo and a few of the boys along to keep an eye on you. And—the first theeng—the *Roumi* cops peek you up. Beeg deal! Ha!"

"This seems to be a case of mistaken identity," Lafayette said reasonably. "I've never seen you before in my life. My name is O'Leary, and I live in the palace with my wife, Countess Daphne, and I don't know what you're talking about!"

"Oh?" the old chieftain said with a sly smile. "O'Leary, eh? You got any ideentification?"

"Certainly," Lafayette said promptly, patting his pockets. "I have any number of . . . documents . . . only . . ." With a sinking feeling, he surveyed the soiled red bandanna his hip pocket had produced. "Only I seem to have left my wallet in my other suit."

"Oh, too bad." King Shosto wagged his head, grinning at his lieutenants. "He left eet een hees other suit." His smile disappeared. "Well, let's see what you've got een *theese* suit to show for a night's work! Show us the trophy that proves your skeel weeth your feengers!"

With all eyes on him, Lafayette rummaged dubiously, came up with a crumpled pack of poisonous-looking black cigarettes, an imitation pearl-handled penknife, a worn set of brass knuckles, a second soiled handkerchief of a virulent shade of green, and a gnawed ivory toothpick.

"I, er, seem to have gotten hold of someone else's coat," he ad-libbed.

"And somebody else's pants," King Shosto grated. "And that somebody ees Zorro!" Suddenly the giant knife was in the old man's hand, being brandished under O'Leary's noise. "Now I cut your heart out!" he roared. "Only eet would be too queek!"

"Just a minute!" Lafayette back-pedaled, was grabbed and held in a rigid grip by eager volunteers.

"The peenalty for failure to breeng home the bacon ees the Death of the Thousand Hooks!" Shosto announced loudly. "I decree a night of loafing and dreenking to get eento the mood, so we do the job right!"

"Zorro! What about your treeck pockets?" a tearful feminine voice cried. The girl who had been showing signs of distress ever since Lafayette's arrival rushed forward and seized his arm as if to tug him from the grip of the men. "Show them, Zorito! Show them you are as beeg a thief as any of them!"

"Gizelle, go bake a pizza!" the old man roared. "Theese is none of your beezness! Theese cowardly peeg, he dies!"

"Eet ees too!" she wailed defiantly. "Theese ees the cowardly peeg I love!"

"*Zut alors!*" Shosto yelled. "You . . . and theese four-flusher! Theese viper een my bosom! Theese upstart! Never weel he have you!"

"Zorito!" she wailed. "Don't you remeember how I steetched all those secret pockets for you, and how you were going to feel theem weeth goodies? Don't you have one leetle souvenir of your treep to show theem?"

25

"Secret pockets?" Shosto rumbled. "What's these nonsense?"

"Een his sleeves!" Gizelle seized Lafayette's cuff, turned it back, explored with her brown fingers. With a yelp of delight she drew forth a slim, silvery watch dangling from a glittering chain.

"You see? Zorito, my hero!" As she flung her arms around Lafayette's neck, Shosto grabbed the watch, stared at it.

"Hey!" the man called Luppo blurted. "You can stuff me for an owl eef that eesn't the solid platinum watch of the Lord Mayor of Artesia Ceety!"

"Where deed you get theese?" Shosto demanded.

"Why, I, ah . . ." Lafayette faltered.

"He stole eet, you brute," Gizelle cried. "What do you theenk, he bought eet een a pawnshop?"

"Well, Shosto, eet looks like Zorro fooled you theese time," someone spoke up.

"He not only leefted the Lord Mayor's watch—but what an actor!" another said admiringly. "I would have sworn he deedn't have the proverbial weendow to throw eet out of—and all the while he had the beegest heist of the decade stashed een hees coat lining!"

"Come on, Shosto—be a sport!" another challenged. "Admeet he had made the team!"

"Well—maybe I geev heem another chance." Shosto dealt himself a blow on the chest that would have staggered a lesser man, grinned a sudden, flashing grin. "Teen thousand thundering devils on a teen roof!" he roared. "Theese ees an occasion for celebration! We proceed weeth the loafing and dreenking as planned! Too bad we have to do weethout the diversion of the Death of the Thousand Hooks," he added, with a regretful glance at Lafayette. "But I can always reschedule eet, eef he doesn't treat my leetle Gizelle right!" He gestured grandly and the men holding Lafayette released him.

The Wayfarers gathered around him, slapping him on the back and pumping his hand. Someone struck up a tone on a concertina; others joined in. Jugs appeared, to be passed from hand to hand. As soon as he could, Lafayette disengaged himself, used the green handkerchief to wipe the sweat from his forehead.

"Thanks very much," he said to Gizelle. "I, uh, appreciate your speaking up for me, miss."

She hugged his arm, looked up at him with a flashing smile. Her eyes were immense, glistening dark, her nose delightfully retroussé, her lips sweetly curved, her cheeks dimpled.

"Theenk nothing of it, Zorito. After all, I couldn't let theem cut you in beets, could I?"

"I'm glad somebody around here feels that way. But I still have the problem of getting home. Could I arrange to borrow a horse—just overnight, of course—"

A burst of laughter from the gallery greeted this request. Gizelle compressed her lips, took Lafayette's arm possessively.

"You are a beeg joker, Zorito," she said sternly; then she smiled. "But eet ees no matter; I love you anyway! Now—on weeth the festeevities!" She seized his hand and whirled him away toward the sound of music.


2


It was three hours later. The twenty-gallon punch-tank contained only half an inch of pulpy dregs; the roast ox had been stripped to the bones. The musicians had long since slid, snoring, under their benches. Only a few determined drinkers still raised raucous voices in old Wayfarer songs. Gizelle had disappeared momentarily on some personal errand. It was now or never.

Lafayette put down the leathern cup he had been nursing, eased silently back into the shadows. No one called after him. He crossed a moonlit strip of grassy meadow, waited again in the shelter of the trees. The drunken song continued undisturbed. He turned and slipped away between the trees.

A hundred feet up the trail, with the sounds and smells of the celebration already lost in the spicy scent of pine and the soughing of wind through the heavy boughs, Lafayette halted, peering back down-trail for signs of followers. Seeing no one, he tiptoed off the trail, setting a direct course for the capital—about ten miles due south, he estimated. A long hike, but well worth it to get clear of this bunch of maniacs. Little Gizelle was the only sane person in camp—and even she had some serious hang-ups. Well, he'd send her a nice memento once he was safely back in town; a string of beads say, or possibly a party dress. It would be nice to see her dolled up. He pictured her garbed in formal court wear, with jewels in her hair and her fingernails polished, and just a touch of perfume back of the ear.

"I might even invite her down to a rout or ball," he mused. "She'd be a sensation, cleaned up a little; she might even meet some nice young fellow who'd put a ring on her finger, and—"

Ducking under a low-spreading branch, Lafayette halted, frowning at a large pair of boots visible under a bush. His gaze traveled upward along a matching pair of legs, surmounted by the torso and unfriendly features of Luppo, standing fists on hips, smiling crookedly down at him.

"Looking for sometheeng, Zorro?'" the big man growled in his husky voice.

"I was just taking a little constitutional," Lafayette said, getting to his feet with as much dignity as he could muster.

"Eef I was the suspeecious type," Luppo growled, "I might theenk you were trying to sneak out on my seester like a feelthy double-crossing rat."

With a muttered "Hmphff," Lafayette turned and made his way back down the path, followed by the big tribesman's sardonic chuckle. Judging that he had put sufficient distance between himself and Luppo, he picked a spot where the undergrowth thinned, again left the path, striking off to the left. A dense stand of brambles barred his path; he angled uphill to avoid it, crawled under a clump of thorn, scaled an outcropping of rock, turned to take his bearings, and saw a large man named Borako leaning against a tree, casually whittling a stick. The Wayfarer looked up, spat.

"Another shortcut?" he inquired with a sly smile.

"Actually," Lafayette said haughtily, "I thought I spotted a rare variety of coot over this way."

"Not a coot," Borako said. "A wild goose, I theenk."

"Well, I can't stand here nattering," Lafayette said loftily. "Gizelle will be wondering where I am."

He made his way back down into camp. Borako's boots clumping behind him. Gizelle met him as he reached the clearing.

"Zorito! Come! Eet's time to get ready for the wedding."

"Oh, is someone getting married?" Lafayette said. "Well, I'm sure it will be a jolly occasion, and I appreciate the invitation, but—" His remonstrances were cut short as Gizelle threw her arms around his neck.

"Uh—Gizelle," he started, "there's something I should tell you—"

"Zorito! Stop talking! How can I keess you?"

"Are you sure you know me well enough?" He temporized as she clung to him.

"Eet ees an old tribal custom," she murmured, nibbling his ear, "to sneak a leetle sample of the goods before buying . . ."

"Buying?" Lafayette stalled. "You mean stealing, don't you?"

Gizelle giggled. "Sure—you get the idea. Come on." She caught his hand and pulled him toward her wagon. As they approached it, a large man stepped forth from the shadows.

"Well—what do you want, you beeg bum?" Gizelle said spiritedly, with a toss of her head.

"The Ancient Law don't say notheeng about geeving the veectim a beeg smooch before the wedding," the man said sullenly.

"So—what's eet to you, Borako?"

"You know I got the hots for you, Gizelle!"

"Get lost you," Lafayette spoke up. "Can't you see you're disturbing the lady?"

"You want to come out een the alley and say that?" Borako demanded, stepping forward truculently.

"No!" Gizelle cried, hurling herself at him; he knocked her roughly aside.

"Here!" Lafayette exclaimed. "You can't do that!"

"Let's see you stop me!" Borako yanked the bread knife from his belt, advanced on Lafayette in a crouch. As he slashed out with the blade, Lafayette leaned aside, clamped a complicated two-handed grip on the man's wrist and with a heave, levered him over his hip. Borako executed a flip and landed heavily on his jaw and lay still, while the knife went skittering across the grass.

"Zorito! My hero!" Gizelle squealed, throwing her arms around Lafayette's neck. "For a meenute there I theenk eet ees all over! But you protected me, at the reesk of your life! You *do* love me, my hero!"

"You did the same for me," Lafayette mumbled, his vocal apparatus somewhat encumbered by the kisses of the grateful girl. "That was queek theenking—I mean, quick thinking—"

"Aha—you sleeped! You forgot your phony accent!" Gizelle hugged him tighter. "Frankly, I was begeening to wonder a leetle . . ."

"Look here," Lafayette said, holding her ar arm's length. "Look at me! Do I really look like this Zorro character?"

"Zorito, you are a beeg comeec!" Gizelle grabbed his ears, nibbled his cheek. "Of course you look like yourself, seely! Why shouldn't you?"

"Because I'm *not* myself! I mean, I'm not anyone named Zorito! I'm Lafayette O'Leary! I'm a peaceful *Roumi,* who just happened to be skulking around in the dark and got picked up by the City Guard, and rescued by mistake by Luppo and his thugs! And now everybody seems to think I'm somebody I'm not!"

Grizelle looked at him doubtfully. "Nobody could look theese much like my Zorito and not be Zorito . . . unless you got maybe a tween brother?"

"No, I'm not twins," Lafayette said firmly. "At least," he started, "not unless you want to count certain characters like Lorenzo and Lothario O'Leary, and of course Lohengrin O'Leary, and Lafcadio and Lancelot—" he caught himself. "But I'm just obfuscating the issue. They don't really exist—at least not in this continuum."

"You sure talk a bunch of nonseense, Zorito," Gizelle said. "Hey—I know! Take off your clothes!"

"Er—do you think we have time?" Lafayette hedged. "I mean—"

"You got a leetle birthmark on your heep," Gizelle explained. "Let me see, queek!"

"Just a minute, somebody might come along and get the wrong idea!" Lafayette protested; but the girl had already grabbed his shirt, yanked the tails clear of his belt, dragged his waistband down to expose his hip bone.

"See? Just like I remember!" she pointed in triumph to the butterfly-shaped blemish on the olive skin. "I knew you were keeding all along, Zorito!"

"That's impossible," Lafayette said, staring at the mark. He poked at it experimentally. "I never had a birthmark in my life! I . . . ." his voice faltered as his gaze focused on his fingertip. It was a long, slender finger, with a grimy, well-chewed nail.

"That," O'Leary said, swallowing hard, "is not my finger!"

"I'm perfectly fine," Lafayette said calmly, addressing the backs of his eyelids. "Pulse sixty, blood pressure normal, temperature 98.6° F., sensory impressions coming in loud and clear, memory excellent—"

"Zorito," Gizelle said, "why are you standeeng there weeth your eyes closed, talking to yourself?"

"I'm not talking to myself, my dear. I'm talking to whoever I've turned into—*whom*ever, I should say—object of the preposition, you know—"

"Zorito—you don't turn into eenybody—you are steel you!"

"I can see we're going to have a little trouble with definitions," Lafayette said, feeling the fine edge of hysteria creeping higher, ready to leap. With an effort, he pulled himself together.

"But as I tried to tell your uncle, I have important business in the capital—"

"More important than your wedding night?"

"*My* wedding night?" Lafayette repeated, dumbfounded.

"Yours—and mine," Gizelle said grimly.

"Wait a minute," Lafayette said, "this has gone far enough. In the first place, I don't even know you, and in the second place I've already got a wife, and—" He leaped back just in time as a slim blade flashed in the girl's hand.

"So—eet's like theese, eh?" she hissed, advancing. "You theenk you can play games weeth the heart of Gizelle? You theenk you can keess and run away, hey? I'll feex you so you never break a poor girl's heart again, you worm-in-the-grass!" She leaped, Lafayette bumped against the side of a wagon; the blade came up—

But instead of striking, Gizelle hesitated. Sudden tears spilled from her long-lashed eyes. She let the stiletto fall from her fingers, covered her face with her hands.

"I can't do eet," she sobbed. "Now they weel all speet

on me, b-b-but I don't care. I weel keel myself instead . . ."

She groped for the knife; Lafayette grabbed her hands.

"No!" he blurted. "Gizelle! Stop! Listen to me! I . . . I—"

"You . . . you do care for me theen?" Gizelle said in a quavering tone, blinking away the tears.

"Of course I care for you! I mean . . ." He paused at the succession of expressions that crossed the girl's piquant face.

"You remeember now how much you love me?" she demanded eagerly.

"No—I mean—I don't remember, but . . ."

"You poor darleeng!" Sudden contrition transformed Gizelle's features into those of an angel of mercy. "Luppo said you got heet on the head! Theese geeves you amnesia, no? That's why you don't remeember our great love!"

"That . . . that must be it," Lafayette temporized.

"My Zorito," Gizelle cooed. "It was for me you got knocked on the head; come, we go eenside; soon eet weel all come back to you." She turned him toward the wagon door.

"But—what if your uncle sees us—"

"Let heem eat hees heart out," Gizelle said callously.

"Fine—but what if he decides to cut *my* heart out instead?"

"You don't have to play cheecken any longer, Zorito; you made your point. Now you get your reward." She lifted a heavy latch and pushed open the door; a candle on a table shed a romantic light on tapestries, icons, rugs, a beaded hanging beyond which was visible a high-sided bed with a red and black satin coverlet and a scattering of pink and green cushions, a tarnished oval mirror. Lafayette stared in fascination at the narrow, swarthy, black-eyed face reflected there. Glossy blue-black hair grew to a widow's peak above high-arched brows. The nose was long and aquiline, the mouth well-molded if a trifle weak, the teeth china-white except for a gold filling in the upper left incisor. It wasn't a bad-looking face, Lafayette thought

33

numbly, if you liked them flashy and heavy on the hair oil.

Hesitantly, he fingered an ear, poked at his cheek, writhed his lips. The mirrored face aped every action.

"Zorito, why are you weegling your leeps?" Gizelle inquired anxiously. "You aren't goeeing to have a feet, are you?"

"Who knows?" he said, with a hollow laugh, fingering a lean but tough biceps. "I seem to be stuck with someone's else's body; it might have anything from paresis to angina pectoris. I suppose I'll find out as soon as the first attack strikes."

"You are a naughty boy, Zorito, not to tell me you are a seek man," Gizelle said reproachfully. "But eet's OK—I'll marry you eenyway. Eet weel be fun while you last." She kissed him warmly. "I won't be a meenute," she breathed as she slid through into the next room with a soft clash of beads.

Dimly through the curtain he saw her toss a garment aside with a deft motion; saw the soft ivory glow of her skin in the colored light.

"Why don't you get comfortable?" she called softly. "And pour us a glass of blackberry wine. Eet's een the cupboard over the Ouija board."

"I've got to get out of here," Lafayette mumbled, averting his eyes from the alluring vision. "Daphne would never understand the Law of the Tribe." He tiptoed to the door, had his hand on the knob when Gizelle's soft voice spoke behind him:

"Seely—that's not the cupboard. The door beside eet!" He turned; she stood in the doorway, clad in an invisible negligee.

"Oh, of course. My amnesia, you know," he jerked his hand back.

"Amnesia, nothing," she snapped. "You don't theenk I ever let eeny man eento my bedroom before, do you?"

"No offense," Lafayette said quickly, forcing his gaze from her figure to the corner of the room.

Gizelle giggled. "Oh, boy, what a surprise eef you'd stepped out there and run eento Borako. The sight of you

34

would drive heem mad weeth jealousy."

"Maybe I'd better just go out and have a word with him," Lafayette suggested.

"Don't overdo the hero routine, my Zorito. Borako ees steel the tribal champ weeth a knife, even eef you deed accidentally treep heem up. Better geev heem time to cool off. . . ." She came to him, slipped her arms around his neck. "Now you better kees me, before *I* cool off, my lover!"

"Ah . . . mmmnnn," Lafayette said as their lips met. "I just remembered something I have to do—"

Gizelle made a swift movement; the knife glittered under Lafayette's nose.

"I theenk you remember the wrong theengs at the wrong time, beeg boy," she said in a tone like a torn metal. "Better geet weeth the program!"

"Do you . . . carry that knife all the time?" O'Leary inquired, edging away from it.

"As long as I have one leetle wisp on to hide eet een," she said sweetly.

"Oh," Lafayette said. "In that case—I mean, ah . . ."

"You forgot the wine," Gizelle said. She brushed past him, took out a purple bottle and two long-stemmed glasses, poured them full.

"To our wedded blees," she murmured and sipped. "What's the matter, you don't dreenk?" she asked sharply as Lafayette hesitated.

"Uh—to wedded bliss," he said, and drank. "And now, why don't we, ah, repair to the, er, nuptial couch?"

Gizelle giggled.

"I'll turn off the light," Lafayette said, and quickly snuffed the candle.

"What's the matter, you don't like to look at me?" Gizelle pouted. "You theenk I'm ugly?"

"I'm afraid of a heart attack," Lafayette said. "Can I, ah, help you with your, er, garment?"

"As you weesh, carissimo," she breathed. Lafayette's fingers brushed satin skin; then he was holding the wispy negligee. Something heavier than sheer silk thumped

35

against his knee; the knife, in a thin leather sheath.

"Now—take me, my Zorito—I am yours!"

"Uh, I'd better make sure the door's locked," Lafayette said, backing away from the sound of her voice.

"Don't worry about trifles at a time like theese!" she whispered urgently. "Where are you, Zorito?"

"How about the back door?" Lafayette persisted, groping in the dark for the doorknob.

"There ees no back door!"

"I'll just make one last check," Lafayette said as his fingers found the latch. He jerked the door open, slid through into bright moonlight, slammed the door and shot home the bolt. From beyond the panel, Gizelle's voice called his name in a puzzled tone. As Lafayette hastily descended the three steep steps, the bulky figure of Borako separated itself from the shadow of a giant tree fifty feet away.

"Ha!" he growled; in the moonlight his teeth flashed white in a wide and unfriendly grin. "Threw you out, deed she? Eet feegures. And now I feex you, permanently." Borako jerked the knife from his belt, whetted it on a hairy forearm, advancing toward Lafayette.

"Look here, Borako," Lafayette said, edging sideways. "I bounced you on your head once today; am I going to have to do it again?"

"Last time you treecked me," Borako snarled. "Theese time I've got a few freends along to referee." As he spoke, three large men materialized from the deep shaodws behind him.

"Well, now that you have a foursome, you can play a few holes of golf," Lafayette snapped. As he spoke, the door of the wagon rattled; a sharp, furious shriek sounded, followed by the pounding of irate feminine fists on the panels.

"Hey—what deed you do to her?" Borako grunted.

"Nothing," Lafayette said. "That's what she's mad about."

As his cohorts rushed to the locked door, Borako uttered a roar and charged. Lafayette feinted, ducked aside and thrust out a foot, hooked Borako's ankle. The Wayfarer plunged headfirst into a wagon wheel, wedging his head firmly between the big wooden spokes.

The other three men were fully occupied in impeding each other's efforts to unbar the door. Lafayette faded back between wagons, turned, and sprinted for the shelter of the deep forest.

# CHAPTER THREE

## 1

For half an hour, the sounds of men beating the brush waxed and waned around O'Leary where he lay facedown in the concealment of what he had belatedly realized was a patch of berry bramble. At length the activity dwindled, a last voice called a final curse. Silence fell. Lafayette crawled forth, dusted himself off, wincing at the impressive variety of aches and pains he had acquired thus far in the night's adventures. He groped inside his coat; the Mark III was still in place. He scanned the dark slope below. Terraced formations of crumbling rock strata led precariously downward.

He started down, keeping his eyes carefully averted from the vista of black treetops beneath him. It was a stiff twenty-minute climb to a wide ledge where he flopped down to rest.

"Out of condition," he told himself disgustedly. "Lying around the palace with no more exercise than a set of lawn tennis now and then is making an old man of me. When I get back, I'll have to start a regimen of dieting and regular workouts. I'll jog early in the morning—say ten laps around the gardens while the dew is still on the roses— then a nice light breakfast—no champagne for a while— then a light workout on the weights before lunch . . ." He paused, hearing a faint sound in the underbrush. A hunting cat? Or Borako and his men, still on the prowl. . . .

Lafayette got to his feet, resumed his cautious descent. The moon went behind a cloud. In pitch darkness, his feet groped for purchase. A rock moved underfoot; he slid, caught at wiry roots, slithered down a sudden steep declivity, fetched up with a painful thump while small stones rattled down around him.

For a moment he lay still, listening for alarums and excursions from above. Except for a high, faint humming as of a trapped insect, the night silence was unbroken.

Lafayette got cautiously to his feet. Inches from the spot where he had fallen, the ledge dropped vertically away; a yard or so on either side of him it curved back in to meet the cliff face.

"Nice going, O'Leary; you've got yourself trapped like a mouse in a wastebasket."

His eyes, accustoming themselves to the darkness, were caught by a faint hint of light emanating from a vertical cleft in the rockface, two feet to the right of the ledge. He leaned out, peered into a narrow, shadowy passage cutting back into the rock, barely visible in the pale glow from an unseen source.

There might be room to squeeze through, he decided. "And maybe there'll be a rear entrance. It's either that, or spend the rest of the night waiting for Borako and Luppo to find me when the sun comes up."

Without further debate, he swung himself out, found a foothold, and squeezed through the narrow opening. A narrow passage led inward ten feet, turned sharply to the right, and debouched into a wide, cool cave bathed in a ghostly blue light.

The rock chamber in which Lafayette found himself was high-vaulted, smooth-floored, with rough-hewn walls. The eerie glow came from an object resting on a pair of trestles in the center of the room—an object that bore an uncomfortable resemblance to a coffin. It was seven feet long, a foot deep, tapering toward each end from the three-foot breadth of its widest point. A remarkable assemblage of wires and pipes led from the foot of the sarcophagus—if it was a sarcophagus—down to a heavy baseplate where an array of dials glowed a bilious yellow from their own inner illumination.

"Just take it easy," Lafayette soothed himself. "There's nothing spooky about it. It's all perfectly natural. Outside the sun will soon be shining. It just happens to be a cave with a box in it, that's all. . . ."

O'Leary circled the coffin—if it *was* a coffin, he reminded himself doggedly, suppressing a tendency for the hairs on the nape of his neck to stand erect. There was nothing else in the chamber; no other passage led from it; there was no sound but the soft hum, like that of a heavy-duty freezer, Lafayette thought.

"A coffin-shaped freezer? Why would anyone want a coffin-shaped freezer?" he inquired aloud in a breezy tone; but the hollow, echoic quality of his words robbed them of the cheeriness he had intended. In silence he approached the box; it was covered by a thick lid, sealed with a strip of sponge rubber. At close range he saw that a layer of dust overlay the smooth, gray-green plastic. Lafayette drew a finger across the surface, leaving a distinct mark that glowed more brightly than the surrounding area.

"The accumulation of a few days—or a few weeks," he assessed. "So whatever this is, it hasn't been here long . . ."

There was a small nameplate attached to the side of the box. Lafayette could barely make out the lettering in the weak light:

## STASIS POD, MARK XXIV
### 220v., 50 amp, 12 HP

Below this terse legend, other words had been carefully defaced, the metal scraped bare. Lafayette felt a deeper excitement stir within him.

"More Central equipment," he murmured. "First the Focal Referent—plus rumors of more of the same in a cave; then this—in another cave. There has to be a connection—and the connection has to tie in with me being somebody I'm not. . . ."

He felt over the plastic case for further clues to its nature; under his hands he could feel a minute vibration, plus a barely perceptible sensation as of electrical current flowing over the surface. His finger encountered a small depression; as he explored it, a soft *click!* sounded from deep inside the container.

At once, the humming sound took on a deeper tone. Lafayette stepped back, startled. Further clickings and snickings as of closing relays came from the box. A sound remarkably like that of a blower motor started up. Lights winked on the panel. Needles stirred and jumped on dials, moving toward red lines.

Lafayette grabbed for the switch he had tripped, poked and prodded at it frantically; but the process he had set in motion proceeded serenely. He searched for another switch; there wasn't one. On all fours, he peered at the instrument faces, but their readings were cryptic:

97.1 SBT; BM 176 . . . 77 . . . 78; NF 1.02; 1AP 15 kpsc.

"Now I've done it," he muttered. Scrambling to his feet, he cracked his head a dizzying blow on the underside of the container. Through the momentary haze, it seemed that the top of the case was slowly sliding back, revealing an interior lined with padded red satin.

"It looks like Dracula's coffin," he mumbled, holding his head in both hands. "It even has . . ." His voice faltered as the retracting cover revealed a pair of feet clad in pointed black shoes. "It even has feet like Dracula . . . and . . ."

Now a pair of purple-clad legs were visible. A long cloak swathed the knees and upper legs. There was a heavy gold chain at the waist. A pair of long-fingered, knuckly hands were folded on the broad chest. From them, rings winked in the gloom. A white beard appeared, clothing an age-lined but powerful chin. A great hawk nose came into view, closed eyes under bushy black eyebrows, a noble sweep of forehead, a purple velvet skullcap atop backswept white locks.

"Not Dracula after all," O'Leary managed. "It's Merlin . . ." He watched in total fascination as the sleeper's chest rose and fell. A finger stirred. The lips parted, uttered a sigh. The eyelids fluttered, opened. Lafayette stared into a pair of immense, violet-pale eyes which fixed on him in a piercing stare.

"I, ah, I'm sorry, sir," O'Leary said hastily. "I just happened along, and I, ah, accidentally seem to have, er, interfered with your arrangements. I hope I haven't caused you any serious inconvenience . . ." As he spoke he backed away, followed by those hypnotic eyes.

"I'll go for help," he said, edging toward the exit, "and before you know it . . ." His voice trailed off as the staring eyes bored fixedly into his. The old man sat up suddenly, an expression of ferocity contorting his noble features. He drew a deep breath, uttered a snorting roar, and lunged—

As if released from paralysis, O'Leary gained the entry in a bound, squeezed into the narrow passage, lost skin thrusting through the cleft. His foot trod air. He grabbed, slipped, yelled—

And was falling through space. For a long moment he was aware of the rush of wind, of the starry canopy wheeling above him—

Then a silent explosion filled the world with Roman candles.

*How lovely,* Lafayette thought dreamily, *to be lying in a big, soft bed, warm and cozy and without a problem in the world.*

*Yes, indeed, a* whispery voice said soothingly. *Now, just relax and let your mind rove back over the events of the last few weeks. Back to your first meeting with him. That was . . . where—*

*With who?* Lafayette inquired offhandedly. *Or with whom?* He wasn't greatly interested. It was so much nicer just to let it all slide away on a sea of black whipped cream . . .

*Tell me!* the voice persisted, more urgently. *Where is he now? And where is it? Speak!*

*Sorry,* Lafayette replied. *I'm not in the mood for riddles right now. Why not go find someone else to play with? I just want to doze a little longer, and then Daphne will bring me a cup of coffee and tell me about all the nice things planned for the day, starting with breakfast on the balcony. . . .*

He paused for a moment in these pleasant reflections to wonder what day it was. Sunday? Possibly—but it didn't seem like Sunday, somehow. And there was something else nagging at the corner of his mind, now that he thought about it. Something he was supposed to do—

He tried to ignore the intruding thought and snuggle back into the dream; but the damage had been done. He was waking up in spite of himself, in spite of a subconscious instinct that told him that the longer he slept the better he'd like it . . .

He opened his eyes, was looking up at a canopy of what appeared to be woven grass and leaves.

"Ah, awake so soon?" a brisk, cheery voice inquired at close range. "What about a spot of breakfast, then?"

Lafayette turned his head; a round, wizened face beamed down at him.

"Who—" Lafayette croaked, and cleared his throat, occasioning a sharp throb at the back of his skull. "Who are you?"

"I? Well, as to that—you may call me Lom. Quite. Good a name as any, what? And what do you say to Bavarian ham, eggs Benedict, oatmeal bread—lightly toasted—with unsalted Danish butter and a spot of lime marmalade; and coffee, of course. It's New Orleans style: I hope you don't mind a bit of chicory?"

"Don't tell me," Lafayette whispered, salivating profusely. "I've died and gone to wherever well-intentioned sinners go."

"Not at all, my dear sir." Lafayette's host chuckled gently. "You've taken a bit of tumble, but we'll soon have you right as rain."

"Fine—but . . . where am I?" Lafayette raised his head, saw the rough walls of a lean-to made of sticks, and beyond the doorway the bright sunshine of a spring morning.

"Why, you're sharing my humble quarters," Lom said. "I apologize for the somewhat primitive accommodations, but one does the best one can with the resources at hand, eh?"

"Haven't we met before? Your voice seems familiar."

"I doubt it—though one can never be sure, eh?" Lom looked quizzically at O'Leary.

"The last thing I remember," Lafayette said, "was falling off a cliff. . . ." He made a move to sit up; pain lanced through his right arm.

"Oh, best you don't move about," the old fellow said quickly. "You've had a nasty fall, you know. But you were fortunate in descending through the tops of a number of trees before coming to rest in a dense fern thicket."

"What time is it?" O'Leary asked. "What day is it?"

"Oh, I should say it's half past ten," Lom said cheerfully. "As for the day . . . ummm. I fear I've lost count.

44

But it was just last night—or more properly, early this morning that I found you. My, what a din you made!"

"Ten thirty. Ye gods, I'm wasting time—" O'Leary made another move to sit up; but Lom pressed him back.

"My dear chap, you mustn't think of venturing out yet! The consequences, I fear, would be most serious!"

"Not half as serious as they'll be if I don't get on my way," O'Leary protested; but he sank back, and Lom turned, lifted a laden tray onto his lap.

"There, now. A bite or two and you'll feel much better."

"Yes, but," Lafayette said, and took a mouthful of softly steaming egg. "Mmnnn hnngg mrrllnggg."

"That's a good chap. Now a bit of the ham, eh?"

"Delicious," Lafayette said, chewing. "But you don't understand, Mr. Lom. I'm not actually what I seem. I mean, things of vast importance are waiting for me to do them." He took a large bite of the hot buttered toast.

"You see, I have to—" he paused; under the mild gaze of the amiable old man, the disclosure he had been about to make sounded too fantastic to voice.

". . . to, ah, attend a certain matters," he said. "After which, I have to, uh, attend to certain *other* matters."

"Of course," the old man nodded in sympathy. "A bit of the marmalade?"

"I don't mean to be mysterious," Lafayette said, accepting the pale-green jelly. "But it's highly classified, you see."

"Ah. Quite candidly, I wondered a bit as to just why you were abroad on the heights; but if you're on official business . . ." Lom smiled understandingly.

"Exactly. Now, how far from town am I?" Lafayette craned to look out through the gaps in the wall. The setting seemed to be one of wild-growing foliage.

"Not far—as the crow flies," Lom said. "But the country between here and the city is somewhat difficult to negotiate, I must confess."

"If you don't mind my asking," Lafayette said, taking a

hearty gulp of coffee, "how do you happen to live here all alone?"

The old man sighed. "True, it's lonely here. But peaceful. The contemplative life has its compensations."

"What do you do when it rains?" Lafayette persisted, noting the gaps in the fronded roof through which patches of bright-blue sky were visible.

"Oh, I take appropriate measures." Lom dismissed the problem with an airy wave of his hand.

"You seem to do very well," Lafayette agreed.

"One becomes accustomed to certain small comforts," Lom said almost apologetically.

"Certainly—I don't mean to pry, Mr. Lom—"

"Just Lom—no Mister. I make no pretensions to wordly titles."

"Oh. Well, Lom, I certainly enjoyed my breakfast, but now I really have to be getting started."

"Nonsense, my boy. You can't stir for at least a week."

"You still don't get the Big Picture, Lom. The future of the kingdom depends on my getting the word through at once."

"I have an idea," Lom said brightly. "Suppose I carry the message for you?"

"That's very kind of you, Lom, but this is much too important to entrust to anyone else." Lafayette lifted the tray aside, sat up, ignoring a swarm of little bright lights that swam into view before him. He swung his legs over the side of the narrow pallet on which he lay, and watched with detached interest as the floor tilted up and struck him a ghostly blow on the head.

". . . . really mustn't!" Lom's voice faded back in. Lafayette was back on the cot, blinking away the obscuring haze. "I can't be responsible for the results!"

"Guess I'm . . . little weaker . . . than I thought," Lafayette panted.

"Indeed, yes. Now about the message: what did you wish me to say?"

"This is noble of you, Lom," Lafayette said weakly.

46

"But you won't regret it. Go directly to Princess Ador-anne—or, no, better if you see Daphne first. That's Countess Daphne O'Leary. The poor girl will be frantic. Tell her where I am, and that—" O'Leary paused. "That, ah, there are certain artifacts—"

"What sort of artifacts?" Lom murmured.

"Sorry, I can't tell you. But anyway, there are these artifacts; tell her they're items Nicodaeus would be especially interested in. And they're hidden . . ."

"Yes?" Lom prompted.

"Well, I can't tell you where. It's sensitive information, you understand. But if she'll get in touch with a . . . a certain party, he can show her where."

"May I ask the name of the certain party?"

"Classified," O'Leary said. "That's about it. Can you remember all that?"

"I think so," Lom said. "Something's hidden somewhere, and someone can tell her where to find it."

"Hmmm. When you put it that way, it doesn't sound like much."

"My boy, face the facts: it sounds like gibberish."

"In that case—I'll have to go myself, ready or not."

"If you'd just be a trifle more explicit . . ."

"Impossible."

"It's equally impossible for you to set out on a journey until you've regained your strength."

"Nevertheless, I'm going."

Lom stroked his chin thoughtfully. "Hmmm. See here, my boy—if you're determined . . . and I see you are . . . of course I wouldn't dream of standing in your way. Now, why don't you give yourself another few minutes' rest—time for your breakfast to digest, can't have you getting stomach cramps—and then I'll speed you on your way."

"All right. I admit I feel a little rocky . . ." Lafayette leaned back and closed his eyes.

"Can't afford to go to sleep," he told himself. "The dizziness will pass as soon as I get on my feet and start moving. Can't be far—should reach a farmhouse in an hour or two—get a ride—be at the palace by early afternoon . . . put call through. . . ."

"Yes?" said the operator. "Central here. Your report, please."

"This is Lafayette O'Leary. I'm calling from Artesia—Locus Alpha Nine-three—"

"I'm sorry, sir. No such locus is listed in the Central Directory. Kindly redial—"

"Wait a minute! Don't ring off! It might take me years to get through to you again! There's an emergency here! It involves a cache of illegal equipment, stolen from Central—"

"No report of missing equipment has been filed, sir. I must now ask you to hang up; the circuits are needed—"

"I've seen it! There's a thing called a Focal Referent—and something else, labeled Stasis Pod! And I have a report of a whole cave full of more of the same!"

"Highly unlikely, sir. You must have made a mistake—"

"I tell you I saw it! In fact, I have the Mark III tucked in a secret pocket inside my coat right now! I know what I'm talking about! I'm an accredited part-time agent of Central! If you don't believe me, talk to Nicholas! He'll tell you!"

"Our records indicate no one of that name in the service."

"Then your records are wrong! He's the one who helped me uncover Goruble's plot to take over the country!"

"Indeed, sir? And what is your name?"

"O'Leary! Lafayette O'Leary! Sir Lafayette O'Leary!"

"Ah, yes. I have a record of that name. . . . But your voice does not agree with the coded pattern listed for Mr. O'Leary—and a visual scan indicates that your face doesn't match the photo of Mr. O'Leary in our files. I must therefore conclude that you are an imposter. The penalty—"

"I'm not an imposter! I just look like one! I can explain!"

"Very well. Explain."

48

*"Well—I can't actually explain, but—"*

*"If you have nothing further to add, sir, I must conclude this conversation now. Thank you for calling . . ."*

*"No! Wait! You have to get the information into the right hands before it's too late! Hello! Hello? Central?"*

Lafayette struggled up from the dream, his shouts echoing in his ears. "Must have dozed off," he mumbled, looking around the hut. Lom was nowhere to be seen. Outside, the light seemed to have taken on a different quality: a late-afternoon quality.

"How long did I sleep?" O'Leary mumbled. He struggled up; he was light-headed, but his legs supported his weight.

"Lom! Where are you—" he called. There was no answer. He stepped outside. The hut—a flimsy shack of sticks and leaves, he saw—was surrounded by a flat clearing no more than a dozen yards in diameter, ringed in by high bushes, beyond which distant peaks rose high into the dusk-tinged sky.

"Ye gods—it's almost dark. I must have slept for hours." Lafayette thrust through the encircling shrubbery—and stopped short. At his feet, a vertical cliff dropped away into dizzying depths. He backed off, checked at another point. In five minutes he knew the worst.

"Marooned," he groaned. "Stuck on top of a mesa. I should have known better than to trust anyone who lives in a grass hut and subsists on Bavarian ham."

Far below, the valley spread, green and orderly, a pattern of tilled fields and winding roads. In the distance, the towers of the palace sparkled, ruddy in the late sun. The nearest of the peaks looming beyond the airy gulf surrounding his eyrie were at least five miles away, he estimated.

"I fell here, eh? From where? And how did that frail little old man carry my one-hundred and seventy-five pounds into his hut unassisted? I must have been crazy not to have smelled treachery." At a sudden thought, Lafayette clutched at his coat.

The Mark III was gone.

"Beautifully handled, O'Leary," he congratulated himself half an hour later, after a fruitless search of the half-acre mesa. "You really came on like a champ every inch of the way. From the minute you got that idiotic note, you've been shrewdness personified. You couldn't have worked yourself into a tighter pocket if it had been planned that way . . ."

He paused to listen to the echo of his own words.

"Planned that way? Of course it was planned that way—but not by you, you dumbbell! The Red Bull must have been in on it; probably someone paid him to con me, and then . . ." his train of thought faltered. "And then—what? Why hijack me, give me somebody else's face, and strand me on a mountaintop?"

"I don't know," he answered. "But let's skip that for now. The important thing is to get off this peak. Lom managed it. I ought to be able to do the same."

"Maybe he used ropes."

"And maybe I'm a kangaroo!"

"Possibly. Have you looked lately?"

Lafayette examined his hands, felt of his features.

"I'm still Zorro," he concluded. "Worse luck."

"And down there, someone is still on the loose with enough Probability gear to shift Artesia into the next continuum. And what are you going to do about it?"

As if in answer to his question, the sky seemed to flicker—like a bad splice in a movie film—and darken; not gradually, but with an abrupt transition from gathering twilight to deep dusk. Some small, fluffy-pink clouds that had been cruising near the adjacent peak were gone, whisked out of sight like dust under a rug. And that wasn't all, O'Leary realized in that same dizzying instant: the peak itself was gone—as were the neighboring peaks. He saw that much before the last of the light drained away, leaving him in total darkness. He took a step back, felt the ground *softening* under his feet. He was sinking down—dropping faster—then falling through black emptiness.

# CHAPTER FOUR

## 1

The wind shrieked past Lafayette's face, buffeted his body. Instinctively, he spread his arms as if to slow his headlong fall. The streaming air tugged tentatively, then with a powerful surge that made the bones creak in his shoulders. In automatic response, he stroked, angling his hands to cup the air. He felt the tug of gravity, the answering lift of giant pinions, sensed the sure, clean speed with which he soared out over darkness.

"Good lord!" he burst out. "I'm flying!"

## 2

The moon came out, revealing a forested landscape far below. For an instant, Lafayette felt a frantic impulse to grab for support; but the instincts he had acquired along with the wings checked his convulsive motion with no more than a sudden, heart-stopping dip in his glide.

"Keep calm," a semi-hysterical voice screamed silently at him from the back of his head. "As long as you keep calm, you'll be all right."

"Fine—but how do I land?"

"Worry about that later."

A lone bird—an owl, Lafayette thought—sailed close, looked him over with cold avian eyes, drifted off on owl business.

"Maybe I can stretch my glide," he thought. "If I can make it back to the capital and reach Daphne . . ." He scanned the horizon in vain for the city lights. Cautiously, he tried to turn, executed a graceful orbit to the left. The dark land below spread to the horizon, unrelieved by so much as a glimmer.

"I'm lost," O'Leary muttered. "Nobody has ever been as lost as this!"

He tried a tentative stroke of his arms, instantly stalled, fell off in a flat spin. He fought for balance, gradually spiraled out into straight and level gliding.

"It's trickier than it looks," he gasped, feeling his heart hammering at high speed under his sternum—or was it just the rush of air? It was hard to tell. Hard to tell anything, drifting around up here in darkness. *Have to get down, get my feet on the ground . . .*

He angled his wings; the horizon slowly rose; the note of the wind in his ears rose to a higher pitch; the buffeting of the air increased.

"So far, so good," he congratulated himself. "I'll just hold my course until I've build up speed, then pull out and . . ." The horizon, he noted, had risen still higher. In fact, he had to bend his neck to see it—and even as he rolled his eyes upward, it receded still further.

"Ye gods, I'm in a vertical dive!" he pressed with his outspread fingers—but it was like thrusting a hand into Niagara Falls.

"There was nothing in *How to Solo Solo* about this," he mumbled, gritting his teeth with the effort. "Why in the world didn't I sprout inherently stable wings while I was at it—"

A tree-covered ridge was rushing toward him with unbelievable swiftness; Lafayette put all his strength in a last-ditch effort. His overstrained wings creaked and fluttered. A dark mass of foliage reared up before him—

53

With a shattering crash, he plunged into a wall of leaves, felt branches snapping—or were they bones?

Someting struck him a booming blow on the head, tumbled him down into bottomless silence.

*How lovely,* Lafayette thought dreamily, *to be lying in a snow bank, dreaming you're in a big, soft bed, warm and cozy, with an aroma of ham and eggs and coffee drifting in from the middle distance. . . .*

He paused for a moment in these pleasant reflections to wonder why it all seemed so familiar. Something was nagging at the corner of his mind: a vague feeling that he'd been through all this before—

*Oh, no, you don't,* he cut the train of thought short. *I know when I'm well off. This is a swell hallucination, and I'm not giving it up without a struggle . . .*

"You've had that thought before, too," the flat voice of experience told him. "It didn't work last time, and it won't work now. You've got problems, O'Leary. Wake up and get started solving them."

*Well, there's one consolation,* he countered. *Whatever my problems are, they're not as silly as what I was dreaming. Wings, already. And a gang of Wayfarers on my trail. And a mummy that came to life, and—*

"Don't look now, O'Leary . . . but you've got a shock coming."

Lafayette pried an eye open. He was looking out through a screen of oversized leaves at a vista of treetops—treetops the size of circus tents, spreading on and on—

He clutched convulsively for support as his eye fell on the curving expanse of rough-textured chocolate-brown bark on which he lay.

"Oh, no," he said. "You've got to be kidding. I didn't *really* crash-land in a treetop after turning into a birdman . . ."

He started to scramble to his feet, felt a stab of pain that started at least ten feet beyond his fingertip and shot like a hot wire all the way up to his neck. Turning his head, he saw a great, sorrel-feathered pinion spread along the wide bough on which he lay, its feathers bedraggled and in disarray. He twitched his shoulder blades tentatively, saw a corresponding twitch of the unfamiliar members, accompanied by another sharp jab of pain—reminiscent of that occasioned by biting down on a bone-chip with a sensitive tooth.

"It's real," he said wonderingly. He sat up carefully, leaned over, looked down through level after level of foot-wide leaves. The ground was down there, somewhere.

"And I'm up here. With a broken wing, Zorp only knows how high in the air. Which means I have to get down the hard way." He studied the two-yard-wide branch under him, saw how it led back among leafy caverns to the shadow-obscured pillar of the trunk.

"It must be fifty feet in diameter. And that's impossible. There are no trees that big in Artesia—or anywhere else, for that matter, especially with leaves like an overgrown sycamore."

"Right," he replied promptly. "Nicely reasoned. The tree's impossible, your wings are impossible, the whole thing's impossible. So what do we do now?"

"Start climbing."

"Dragging a broken wing?"

"Unless you have a better idea."

"Take your choice, O'Leary," he muttered. "Try it, and fall to your death, or stay here and die in comparative comfort."

"Correction," he reminded himself. "You can't afford to be dead—not while the Red Bull is itching to sell Goruble's hoard to any unsavory character with the price of a chicken dinner."

"Besides which," he agreed, "I have a few chicken dinners to eat yet myself."

"That's the spirit. Up and at 'em. *I saye and I doe.*"

Painfully, Lafayette got to his feet, favoring the injured member. The wings, he saw by craning his neck, sprouted from his back between his normal shoulders and the base of his neck. His chest was puffed out like that of a pigeon; hard muscle, he found, prodding himself with the long,

55

lean fingers he now possessed. His face—insofar as he could determine by feeling it over—was narrow, high cheek-boned, with small, close-set eyes and a widow's peak of bushy hair. Somehow, without a mirror, he knew that it was glossy black, that his eyes were a lambent green, his teeth snowy white in a sun-dark face.

"Good-bye, Zorro," he muttered. "It was a mixed pleasure being you. I wonder who I am now? Or what?"

There was a flutter among the leaves, a sharp *kwee, kwee!* A small white bird swooped on him. Lafayette batted at it in surprise, almost lost his balance, yelped aloud at the stab from his wing as he grabbed for support. The bird hovered, *kwee*ing in a puzzled way. A moment later two more joined in. Lafayette put his back to a branch, fended off their repeated attempts to dart in close.

"Get away, blast you!" he yelped. "Don't I have enough trouble without being pecked by meat-eating cockatoos?"

More birds arrived; squawking indignantly, they circled Lafayette's head. He backed along the branch; they followed. He reached the giant bole. A dozen or more of the birds fluttered around him now.

"At least wait till I'm dead!" he yelled.

There was a sudden, shrill whistle from near at hand.

Abruptly, the birds flew up, scattering. The branch trembled minutely under Lafayette's feet. Leaves stirred; a small, slender figure stepped into view, swathed in a cloak of feathers—

No, not a cloak, O'Leary corrected his first startled impression.

Wings.

It was another flying man who stood facing him from ten feet away.

The man was narrow-shouldered, narrow-faced, with a long, pointed nose, tight lips, peaked eyebrows above pale, glistening eyes. He was dressed in close-fitting green trousers, a loose tunic of scarlet decorated with gold loops at the cuffs. His feet were bare; his long, slim toes clutched the rough bark.

*"It ik ikik;riz izit tiz tizzik ik?"* the newcomer said in a reedy, musical voice.

"Sorry," Lafayette said, and felt the awkwardness of the word on his lips. "I don't, uh, savvy your lingo . . ."

*"Thib, it ik ikik;rzi izit tiz tizzk ik, izyik!"* The flying man's tone was impatient—but Lafayette hardly noticed that. With one part of his mind he had registered only a series of whistling, staccato sounds—but with another, he had heard words:

"I said, what's the matter? Been eating snik berries?"

"No," Lafayette said, and felt his mouth shape the sound: *"Nif."*

"I thought maybe the zik-zik's had spotted a zazz-worm," the message came clearly through the buzzing and clicking.

"I thought they were trying to eat me alive," O'Leary said—and heard himself mouthing the same twittering sounds.

"Do you feel all right, Haz?" The flying man came forward, moving quickly, with a precise, mincing gait. "You sound as if you had a mouthful of mush."

"As a matter of fact," O'Leary said. "I don't feel too well. I'm afraid heights make me dizzy. Could you, ah, show me the quickest way down?"

"Over the side, what else?" The flying man stared curiously at Lafayette; his eyes strayed to O'Leary's wing, which he had propped against the bole for support.

"Hey—it looks like—good night, fella, why didn't you say so? That's a broken freeble-bone, or I'm a landlubber!"

"I guess," Lafayette said, hearing his voice echo from far away. "I guess . . . it is . . . at that . . ."

He was only dimly aware of hands that caught him, voices that chirped and whistled around him, of being assisted along the rough-textured path, of being lifted, pulled, or twinges from his injury, faint and far away; and then of a moment of pressure—pressure inside his bones, inside his mind, an instant of a curious vertigo, of the world turned inside out . . .

Then he was in cool darkness and an odor of camphor, sinking down on a soft couch amid murmurings that faded into a soft green sleep.


4


"That's three times," he was saying as he awoke. "My skull can't take much more of it."

"Of what, Tazlo darling?" a soft, sweet voice whispered.

"Of being hit with a blunt instrument," O'Leary said. He forced his eyes open, gazed up at a piquant feminine face that looked down at him with an expression of tender concern.

"Poor Tazlo. How did it happen? You were always such a skillful flyer . . ."

"Are you really here?" Lafayette asked. "Or are you part of the dream?"

"I am here, my Tazlo." A soft, slim-fingered hand touched Lafayette's cheek gently. "Are you in much pain?"

"A reasonable amount, considering what I've been through. Strange. I go along for months at a time—even years—without so much as a mild concussion—and then bam—slam—bash! They start using my head for a practice dummy. That's how I can tell I'm having an adventure. But I really can't take much more of it."

"But you're safe now, Tazlo dear."

58

"Ummmnn." He smiled lazily up at the girl. "That's one of the compensations of an active life: these delightful fantasies I have while I'm waking up."

He looked around the room: it was circular, with vertical-grained wood-paneled walls, a dark polished floor; a lofty ceiling, lost in shadows, through which a single shaft of sunlight struck. The bed on which he lay had a carved footboard, a downy mattress, comfortable as a cloud.

"I suppose in a minute I'll discover I'm impaled on a sharp branch a hundred yards over a gorge filled with cacti or crocodiles," he said resignedly, "but at the moment, I have no complaints whatever."

"Tazlo—please . . ." There was a stifled sob in her voice. "Speak sensibly; tell me you know me—your own little Sisli Pim."

"Are you a Sisli Pim, my dear?"

"I'm Sisli Pim, your Intended! You don't remember me!" The elfin face pucked tearfully; but with an effort, she checked the flood, managed a small smile. "But you can't help that, I know. It's the bump on your head that makes you so strange."

"Me, strange?" Lafayette smiled indulgently. "I'm the only normal thing in this whole silly dream—not that you're silly, er, Sisli. You're quite adorable—"

"Do you really think so?" She smiled enchantingly. In the dim light Lafayette thought her hair looked like feathery plumes, pale violet, around her heart-shaped face.

"I certainly do. But everything else is typical of these fantasies I have when I'm waking up. Like this alleged language I'm speaking: it's just something my subconscious made up, to fit in with the surroundings—just gibberish, but at the moment it seems to make perfectly good sense. Too bad I can't get a tape recording of it. It would be interesting to know if it's actually a self-consistent system, or just a bunch of random sounds."

"Tazlo—please don't! You frighten me! You . . . you don't even sound like yourself!"

"Actually, I'm not," O'Leary said. "I'm actually a

59

fellow named Lafayette O'Leary. But don't be frightened, I'm harmless."

"Tazlo—you mustn'tl" Sisli whispered. "What if Wizner Hiz hears you?"

"Who's he?"

."Tazlo—Wizner Hiz is the Visioner of Thallathlonel He might not understand that you're just raving because of a blow on the head! He might take this talk of being someone else seriously! Remember what happened to Fufli Hun!"

"I'm afraid it's slipped my mind. What did happen to poor old Fufli?"

"They . . . Sang him Out."

Lafayette chuckled. "Sisli, anyone who's sat through a concert of the Royal Artesian Philharmonic isn't afraid of any mere choral group." Lafayette sat up, felt a sharp pain in the small of his back—a pain that seemed to originate from a point in midair, two feet above and to the left of his shoulder blade. He twisted his head, saw a bale of white bandages from which rather bedraggled russet feathers protruded.

"What—are *you* still here?"

"Who?" Sisli said in alarm. "Tazlo, you're not seeing invisible enemies, are you?"

"I'm talking about these infernal wings," Lafayette said. "I dreamed I flew through the air with the greatest of ease—until I crash-landed in a treetop. Then there was something about being attacked by meat-eating pigeons —and then a birdman arrived, and . . . and that's all I remember." He rubbed his head. "Funny—by now I should be waking up and having a good laugh about the whole thing . . ."

"Tazlo—you *are* awake! Can't you tell? You're here—in Thallathlone, with me!"

"And before the flying sequence," Lafayette went on, frowning in deep thought, "there was the business of being marooned on a mountaintop. A pretty obvious symbolism, reflecting my feeling of isolation with my problem. You see, I'd found this Focal Referent—some kind of probability gadget, I think, stolen from Central—and I was having a terrible time trying to get word to the authorities—"

"Tazlo—forget all that! It was just a nightmare! Now you're awake! You're going to be fine—just as soon as your wing heals!"

"I find that if you run over a dream in your mind as soon as you wake up, you can fix it in your conscious memory. Now, let's see: there was the man in the cave—*that* was spooky! He was under an enchantment, I suppose—except that the logical part of my mind cooked up something called a Stasis Pod to rationalize things. He represents Widsom, I suppose—but the way he attacked me suggests that I must have a suppressed fear of knowledge."

"Tazlo—why don't we step outside and get a little sunlight, maybe that will dispel these morbid fancies—"

"Just a minute; this is pretty interesting. I never knew you could psychoanalyze yourself just by dissecting your dreams. I always thought I approved of Science—but apparently it's a secret bugaboo of mine. Now, let's see—there was a little old man, too—a cherubic type, he found me after I fell over the cliff, and brought me home and gave me a marvelous breakfast." Lafayette smiled at the recollection. "At the time it didn't even seem strange that someone living in a grass hut would have a refrigerator full of gourmet items—"

"Are you hungry, Tazlo? I have a lovely big boolfruit, just picked."

"Sure, why not?" Lafayette grinned indulgently at the girl. "I may as well sample everything this dream provides—including you . . ." He caught her hand, pulled her to him, kissed her warmly on the mouth.

"Tazlo!" She stared into his eyes with a look of amazed delight. At close range he could see the velvety-smooth texture of her cheek, the long lashes that adorned her pale-green eyes, the downy feathers that curled on her smooth forehead . . . "You mean—you really mean—"

"Mean what?" Lafayette said absently, noting for the first time the graceful white pinions which enfolded Sisli like a glistening feather cloak.

"That—you want to marry me!"

"Wait a minute," Lafayette said, smiling. "Where did you get that idea?"

"Why, you . . . you kissed me, didn't you?"

"Well, certainly, who wouldn't? But—"

"Oh, Tazlo—this is the most wonderful moment of my life! I must tell father at once!" She jumped up, a slim, elfin creature aglow with happiness.

"Wait a minute—let's not bring anyone else into this dream. I like it just the way it is!"

"Father will be so happy! He's always hoped for this day! Good-bye for a moment, my dearest—I'll be right back!" Sisli turned, was gone. Lafayette tottered to his feet, grunted at a pang from his bandaged wing, stumbled after her—and slammed into a solid wall.

He backed off, groped over the rough-hewn wood surface, looking for the door through which Sisli had left.

"It's got to be here," he muttered. "I saw her with my own eyes—or at least with the eyes I happen to be using at the moment . . ." But five minutes' search disclosed no opening whatever in the seamless walls.

"My boy!" a whistling nasal voice exclaimed behind him; he whirled; a gnarled, wizened ancient stood in the center of the room, his face beaming in a toothless smile. "My little girl has just given me the happy tidings! Congratulations! I give my consent, of course, dear lad! Come to my arms!" The old boy rushed forward to embrace Lafayette, who stared in bewilderment over the old fellow's featherless skull at a pair of muscular youths who had appeared silently and stood with folded arms and expressions of slightly bored indulgence, flanking Sisli Pim.

"Father says we can have the ceremony this very evening, Tazlo!" she cried. "Isn't that marvelous?"

"Things are going too fast," Lafayette said. "You're leaping to conclusions," he paused, noting the sudden hostility in the expressions of the two young fellows—probably her brothers, O'Leary decided.

"About what?" one of them demanded.

"I mean—I'm very fond of Sisli, of course—but—"

"But what?" the other youth snapped.

"But I can't—I mean—well, confound it, I can't marry her—or anyone else!"

"Eh? What's this?" the oldest chirped, rearing back to gaze up at Lafayette with eyes as sharp as talons. "Can't marry my daughter?" Sisli Pim uttered a wailing cry. The two brothers stepped forward threateningly.

"What I mean is—I'm not eligible!" Lafayette blurted, backing a step.

"Not eligible—how?" the old man inquired, his gaze impaling O'Leary.

"You own the requisite number of acorns, right?" one of the young men demanded.

"And you have an adequate nest, right?" the other pressed.

"And you *did* kiss her," the first pointed out.

"And she didn't knife you," said his companion. "Which means she accepts you, right?"

"So what could possibly stand in your way?" the old man crowed, as if the problem were solved.

"It's just that . . . that . . ."

"Tazlo—you haven't . . . haven't . . . you didn't—"

"You don't mean, I suppose, that you've contracted an understanding with some other maid of Thallathlone?" the larger brother asked in an ominous tone.

"Certainly not! But I can't ask Sisli Pim to marry me," Lafayette said flatly. "I'm sorry I kissed her. I didn't mean it."

There was a sudden movement, a whistle of steel on leather, and a knife was poking Lafayette's throat, gripped in the hard, brown fist of the smaller of the brothers.

"Sorry you kissed my sister, eh?" he hissed.

"No—as a matter of fact I'm *not* sorry," Lafayette snapped, and stamped down hard on the knife-wielder's instep, at the same time chopping outward at the offending wrist, while ramming a fist into the youth's ribs. The lad doubled over, coughing and hopping on one foot.

"As a matter of fact I enjoyed it a lot," O'Leary said defiantly. "But the fact is, I never saw Sisli in my life before ten minutes ago. How can you want her to marry a stranger?"

"Never saw—" the old man quavered, waving back the other brother. "What can you mean? You were raised together! You've seen each other almost daily for the past twenty-one years!"

"Father—I think I understand," Sisli cried, thrusting herself between Lafayette and her male relatives. "Poor Tazlo feels it wouldn't be fair to marry me, in his condition!"

"Condition? What condition?" Father said querelously.

"In the fall—when he broke his wing—he suffered a blow on the head, and he's lost his memory!"

"A likely tale," the elder brother growled.

"How did he happen . . . unh . . . to fall in the first place?" the younger brother grunted, massaging his stomach, wrist and shin simultaneously.

"Yes—how did you happen to fall, Tazlo—you of all people?" the old man asked. "An expert wingsman like you."

"It's a long story," Lafayctte said shortly. "You wouldn't understand—"

"Please—how can he tell you?" Sisli protested. "He remembers nothing."

"He remembered how to kiss unsuspecting young females," the younger brother growled.

"Look, fellows—why don't you just forget that? It was a mistake, I admit it. I'm sorry if I caused any misunderstanding—"

"Misunderstanding? This silly goose came rushing up to us, blurted out the glad tidings where half the eyrie heard her! We'll all be a laughingstock—especially if we go off and leave you here in her chamber, unchaperoned!"

"Well, then, I'll go elsewhere. I'm not looking for trouble. Just direct me to the nearest telephone—"

"Nearest what?" three voices chimed as one.

"Well, telegraph station, then. Or police station. Or bus

station. I have to get a message through——"

"What's he talking about?"

"He must be raving."

"I think Wizner Hiz ought to know about this."

"No! Tazlo hasn't done anything!" Sisli spoke up. "He'll be fine—just as soon as you go away and leave us alone!"

"Not likely," Younger Brother said grimly. "You come with us, girl—and I'll see to it Haz is moved to a bachelor nest——"

"He needs me! Now get out—both of you—and Father, if you side with them——"

"I never take sides," the old man said quickly. "Calmly, my child. We'll take the matter under advisement. Something will have to be done. In the meantime—suppose we simply keep the entire matter, ah, confidential, eh? No need to give sharp tongues fodder to gnaw on."

"Then you'll have to leave Tazlo here," Sisli said flatly. "If he leaves, everyone will know that . . . that something's amiss."

"Bah, the chit is right," the Younger Brother said.

"Tazlo—hadn't you best lie down?" Sisli said, taking Lafayette's hand.

"I'm fine," Lafayette said. "But they're right. I can't stay here." He turned to the three male members of the family—except for himself and Sisli, the room was empty.

"Where did they go?"

"Umm." Sisly looked thoughtful. "Father's hurrying along to his uncle Timro's perch, probably to discuss the situation over a cup or two of bool cider; and Vugdo and Henbo are standing about twenty feet away, talking. I don't think they're too well pleased. But you know that as well as I, Tazlo."

"How did they get out?"

"They just . . . went, of course. What do you mean?"

"I looked for a . . . door," Lafayette stumbled over the word. "I can't find one."

"What's a *dooor*, Tazlo?"

"You know: the part of the wall that moves—swings out, or slides sideways. I can't seem to think of the word for it in Thallathlonian."

Sisli looked interested. "What's it for, Tazlo? Just decoration, I suppose—"

"It's to get in and out by. You know A *door!*"

"Tazlo—you don't need a *dooor*—whatever that is—to go out. I think that bump on your head—"

"All right then: how do you go out without a door?"

"Why—like this . . ." Sisli turned to the wall and stepped to it—*through* it. Lafayette saw her advancing foot sink into the solid wood, followed by her body, the tips of her trailing wings disappearing last, leaving the wall as unbroken as before. He jumped after her, ran his hands over the grainy wood. It was solid, slightly warm to touch—

Sisli reappeared just under his chin, bumped him lightly as he jumped back. She laughed, rather uncertainly.

"How—how in the world did you do that?" he gasped.

"Tazlo—you *are* just playing a game, aren't you—"

"Game? The game of going out of my mind—" Lafayette caught himself, drew a breath, managed a shaky laugh of his own.

"I keep forgetting. I'd just about decided this was all real instead of a dream. Then you walk through a wall and spoil the illusion. But it's really time I woke up." He slapped his cheeks lightly. "Come on, O'Leary—wake up! Wake up!"

"Tazlo!" Sisli caught his wrists. "Please—stop acting like one who's lost his wits! If Wizner Hiz should see you—terrible things would happen!"

"I've always had this trouble with too-vivid dreams," Lafayette said. "And it's been worse since I read all those books on mesmerism and hypnogogia. If Central didn't have a Suppressor focused on me, I'd be tempted to think I'd been transferred into another probability continuum—"

"Please, Tazlo," Sisli wailed. "Why don't you lie down and have another nice nap—"

"That's just the trouble, Sisli: I'm asleep now, and

dreaming you. I have to wake up and get busy saving the kingdom—"

"Save what kingdom? Thallathlone isn't a kingdom—it's a limited mythocracy!"

"I'm talking about Artesia. It's a bit old-fashioned in some ways, but all in all a very nice place. I used to be a king there—at least I was for a few days, until I could abdicate in favor of Princess Adoranne. That was after I killed Lod, the two-headed giant, and his pet dragon. It wasn't really a dragon, of course, just an allosaurus Goruble had transferred in from a primitive locus—and—"

"Tazlo—lie down, just close your eyes and all these wild fancies will evaporate!"

"They're not wild fancies. *This* is the wild fancy. Don't you see how ridiculous it all is? People with wings, who walk through walls? Typical dream-images, probably reflecting a subconscious wish on my part to be freed of all restraints—"

"Tazlo—*think!* Of course we have wings! Otherwise how could we fly? And of course we walk through walls; how else would we get outside?"

"That's just it—it has all the illogical internal logic of a well-organized dream."

"All that talk about giants and dragons—*that's* the fantasy, Tazlo—don't you see that? They're symbols of the obstacles you feel you have to overcome; and that bit about being a king—a transparent wish-fulfillment. By imagining you abdicated, you have all the prestige of royalty without the responsibilities."

"Say—you know the jargon pretty well yourself. But I suppose that's to be expected, if you're a creation of my subconscious."

Sisli stamped her foot. "*Your* subconscious! Tazlo Haz, I'll have you know that I'm real, live, three-D, living-color female, and your subconscious has nothing to do with it!" She threw her arms around Lafayette's neck, kissed him long and warmly.

"There!" she gasped. "Now tell me I'm your imagination!"

"But—but if you're real," Lafayette stammered, "then ... what about Artesia—and the Red Bull and the cave full of gimmicks, and the old man in the coffin, and Lom, and—"

"Just something you dreamed, Tazlo dear," Sisli murmured. "Now lie down and let me feed you some cold boolfruit, and we'll talk about our future."

"Well . . ." Lafayette hesitated. "There's just one thing." He eyed the blank walls that encircled him. "It's all very well for you to walk through solid wood—and your pop and brothers, too, it seems. But what about me? How do *I* get outside?"

"Tazlo, Tazlo—you've been walking through walls since you were a year and a half old!"

"I guess that's about when I learned to walk—but not through teak paneling."

"Silly boy. Come . . . I'll show you." She took his hand, led him to the wall, slid into it. Lafayette watched as the wood engulfed her flesh, her body merging with the wall as if she were sinking into opaque water. Only her arm protruded, holding his hand. It withdrew swiftly, the wood closing about her forearm, her wrist—

Lafayette's fingers rammed the wood with a painful impact. Sisli's hand still gripped his; she tugged again. He pulled away, was rubbing his skinned knuckles as she reappeared, a worried expression in her wide eyes.

"Tazlo—what's the matter?"

"I told you I couldn't walk through walls!"

"But—but, Tazlo—you *have* to be able to!"

"Facts are facts, Sisli."

"But— if you can't walk through the wall . . ." Her expression was frightened.

"Then I guess I'll have to chop my way out. Can you get me an ax?"

"An *ax?*"

He described an ax.

"There's nothing like that in Thallathlone. And if there were—how long would it take you to cut through six feet of solid kreewood? It's harder than iron!"

68

Lafayette sank down on the bed. "Great. I'm trapped here. But—how did they get me inside—"

Before Sisli could answer, Vugdo—the younger brother—stepped through the wall.

"I've just had a chat with Wizner Hiz," he said. "Now, don't get upset with me," he added as Sisli whirled on him. "He sought me out, asked me how Haz was. I told him he was all right. So . . . he wants to see him."

"Vugdo—how could you?" Sisli wailed.

"He'll have to face him sooner or later. And the sooner the better. If Haz does anything to rouse the old devil's suspicions—well, you know how Wizner is."

"How . . . how soon does he want to see him?"

"He said right now; tonight."

"No!"

"But I stalled him off—until tomorrow morning. I said he had a headache." Vugdo gave Lafayette a sour look. "I didn't tell him his headache is nothing compared with the headache I've got."

After Vugdo had left, Sisli looked at Lafayette with wide, fearful eyes.

"Tazlo—what can we do?"

"I don't know, kid," Lafayette said grimly. "But we'd better get busy doing it."

# CHAPTER FIVE

## 1

"Let's start at the beginning and see if we can make some sense out of this," Lafayette said in a calm, reasonable tone. "Now, I was safe at home, perfectly contented, when I got the note from the Red Bull—"

"Wrong," Sisli said with a shake of her head that made the violet plumes wave adorably. "You were off on one of your hunting expeditions, determined to bring home a pair of gold-crested wiwi-birds to be our hearth-companions after we've set up our nest."

"Very well—if you say so. So I *dreamed* I was in Artesia, getting a note from the Red Bull. And on impulse I did as he asked; went out alone, in the middle of the night, for a mysterious rendezvous at the Ax and Dragon."

"If you were so content—in this dream," Sisli said, "why did you do anything as silly as that?"

Lafayette sighed. "I guess I've always had a romantic streak," he confessed. "Just when everything is at it's best, I get this restless urge to adventure. And I suppose the idea of going back to the Ax and Dragon had something to do with it. That's where it all started, you know—"

"No—I don't know. Tell me."

"Well—where should I begin? Back in Colby Corners, USA, I suppose. I was a draftsman. I worked at the foundry. It wasn't very challenging work. But I used to do a lot of reading. I read up on hyponotism. One evening I was trying out a few of the techniques I'd picked up from Professor Shimmerkopf's book, and . . . well, there I was, in Artesia, walking down a cobbled street in the twilight, with the smell of roast goose and stout ale coming from this tavern—the Ax and Dragon."

"In other words—you admit Artesia was imaginary!" Sisli said triumphantly.

"Well . . . I suppose in terms of Colby Corners and the foundry and Mrs. McGlint's Clean Rooms and Board it was a dream—but once I was there, it was as real as Colby Corners had ever been—realer! I was having adventures, doing all the things I'd always dreamed of doing, having the kind of adventures I'd always wanted—"

"Wish-fulfillment—"

"Please—stop saying 'wish-fulfillment.' I can't remember wishing I was accused of kidnapping the Princess and thrown in jail—or lost in the desert—or locked in a torture cage by Lod."

"But you escaped from all these dilemmas?"

"Well—certainly. If I hadn't, I wouldn't be here. In fact, I'm not sure I *am* here. How can I be sure? A dream seems real while you're dreaming it. You can pinch yourself—but you can dream you pinched yourself—and even dream you woke up, and—"

"Tazlo—please—don't let yourself get so excited. You were telling me about your dream-world of Artesia. . . ."

"Yes. Well, I ended up living in the palace as a sort of permanent guest of Princess Adoranne—"

"This Princess—was she pretty?"

"Incredible. Golden hair, big blue eyes—"

"Blue eyes? How grotesque."

"Not at all; on the contrary. And a figure like an angel—"

"You—you were in love with this creature?"

"Well—I thought I was for a while—but . . ."

"But? But what?"

"But," Lafayette temporized, suddenly noting the edge Sisli's voice had acquired, "but of course in the end I

71

realized I wasn't really in love with her—so she married Count Alain and lived happily ever after—at least for a while."

"While you occupied luxury quarters in her palace. How cozy."

"Believe me, she and I were good friends, that's all. And Count Alain was rated the top swordsman in the kingdom, by the way—"

"So—it was only fear of this redoubtable warrior that kept you from her?"

"Who, Alain? Nonsense. I fought a duel with him once and won—with a little help from Daphne, of course—"

"Who," Sisli said coldly, "is Daphne?"

"Why, Daphne is . . . is the former upstairs maid," Lafayette amended his statement. "But I mustn't get distracted from trying to figure out what's real and what isn't," he hurried on. "Anyway, there I was in Artesia, meeting the Red Bull. I thought—well, I thought it would be like old times, but somehow it wasn't. Even the Red Bull seemed different, somehow—he didn't seem to have any conscience anymore—"

"Things are always changed around in dreams, Tazlo."

"I suppose so. But that wasn't the biggest change. The Red Bull stepped out back for a moment, and suddenly—well, this part is very hard to explain. But suddenly—I was somebody else."

"It happens all the time in dreams," Sisli said sympathetically. "But now you're awake, and yourself, the same dear Tazlo Haz you've always been—"

"But I haven't always been Tazlo Haz! I was Zorro the Wayfarer!"

"I thought you said you were Lafayette Something, ex-king of Artesia! You see, Tazlo, how these different hallucinations keep shifting around?"

"You don't understand. It's all perfectly simple. First I was Lafayette O'Leary—then I was Zorro—and now I'm Tazlo Haz—only I'm still Lafayette O'Leary, if you know what I mean."

"No," Sisli sighed. "I don't. And this isn't helping our

problem, Tazlo. You still have to remember how to walk."

Lafayette sat on the edge of the bed, gripping his head in both hands, ignoring the curious feel of short, curled feathers where his hair should have been.

"I have to come to grips with this," he told himself firmly. "Either I'm awake, and this is real, and I have amnesia—in which case I've always been able to walk through walls—or I'm asleep and dreaming—and if I'm dreaming, I ought to be able to dream anything I want to—such as the ability to walk through walls!" He looked up with a pleased expression.

"Ergo—either way, I can do it." He stood, eyed the wall defiantly, strode to it—and banged his nose hard enough to bring out a shower of little bright lights.

"Oh, Tazlo—not like that!" Sisli wailed. She clung to him, making soothing sounds. "Is it my itty bitty boy, can't even walk, poor Taz, there, there, Auntie Sissy will help . . ."

"I can walk through walls!" Lafayette snapped. "It's a perfectly natural thing to do in this crazy mixed-up place! And I have to do is hold my mouth right, and—" As he spoke, he had disengaged himself from the girl, advanced on the wall—and thumped it hard enough to stagger him.

"Tazlo—you're going about it all wrong!" Sisli cried. "There's really nothing difficult about it, once you get the feel of *merging*."

"Merging, eh?" Lafayette said grimly. "All right, Sisli—you want to help—teach me how to merge. . . !"

2

Lafayette had lost count of the hours. Twice Sisli had gone out for food—birdseed cakes and cups of sweet juices which in spite of their insubstantiality seemed to satisfy the inner man—or the inner whatever-he-was, Lafayette thought sourly. Once Vugdo had appeared, ready to lay down the law, but Sisli had driven him off with a flash of temper that surprised O'Leary. But he was no nearer to pushing his body through six inches of kreewood than he had been at the start.

"Now, Tazlo," the girl said with a gentle patience that Lafayette found touching even in his frustration, "relax, and we'll try again. Remember, *it's not difficult*. It's not anything that requires a tremendous effort, or any special skill. It's all . . . all just a matter of thinking about it in the right way."

"Sure," Lafayette said dully. "Like describing the difference between mauve and puce to a blind man."

"I can remember—just barely—the first time I did it," she said, musingly. Lafayette could sense the bone-deep fatigue in her, see it in the deep shadows under her eyes, the slump of her slim shoulders. But in the soft light from the glow-jar on the table, she still smiled lovingly at him.

"I was almost two. Father and mother had planned a treetop picnic. They'd told me so many times how it would be to see the outdoors for the first time—"

"The first time? At age two?"

"Of course, my Tazlo. An infant can't leave the nest in which it's born until it leans to merge."

"Ye gods. What if the kid can't learn—like me?"

"Then—then it remains a prisoner for life. But that won't happen, Tazlo—it can't happen to you—to us!" Her voice broke into a sob.

"Now, now, take it easy, kid," Lafayette soothed, holding her frail, feather-like figure close to him and patting her back. "I'll catch on after a while—"

"Of . . . of course you will. I'm being silly." She brushed a tear away and smiled up at him. "Now, let's start again. . . ."

The gray light of dawn was filtering through the light-aperture high in the wooden wall against which Lafayette slumped, fingering the newest bruise on his jaw.

"I guess maybe I wasn't meant for merging," he said wearily. "I'm sorry, Sisli. I tried. And you tried. You tried as hard as anyone could try—but—"

"Tazlo—if you don't appear for your appointment with Wizner Hiz, he'll know something is wrong. He'll come here—he'll question you—and when he learns you remember nothing of your life—that you have these strange delusions of other worlds—then he'll—he'll—" Her voice broke.

"Maybe not. Maybe I can convince him I'm just a nut case. That my brains are scrambled. Maybe he'll give me more time—"

"Never! You know how he is about anything that even hints at a Possession!"

"No—how is he?"

"Tazlo—you can't have forgotten *everything*!" Sisli sat beside him, caught his hands, clasped them tightly. "In his Visioning, if he sees anything—just the faintest hint that a Mind-gobbler has gotten a foothold in someone—Out he goes!"

"Out where?"

"Out—outside. Into the Emptiness. *You* know."

"Sisli, could we accept it as a working hypothesis that I *don't* know? You tell me."

"Well . . . it seems so silly to be telling you what everyone knows—but—once, many years ago, Thallathlone was invaded by creatures too horrible to describe. They took people's minds—grabbed them when they had lowered the Barriers so they could merge—and possessed them. At first, the victim would simply seem a little strange—as if he'd . . . lost his memory. But little by little, they began to . . . change. First, they'd start to lose their feathers; their bones would begin to grow; their plumage fell out, and wiry, thin hairs grew in its place. Finally, their wings would—would wither away, and . . . and drop off!"

"It sounds awful," Lafayette said. "But surely that's just a myth. People don't just turn into other people—" he broke off abruptly at the import of what he was saying. "I mean—not usually . . ."

"Exactly," Sisli said. "*I* know you're still really you, Tazlo dear—but . . . but it does look rather . . . rather strange—and to Wizner Hiz, it will look more than strange! He'll be sure you're a Mind-gobbler—and he'll . . . he'll Sing you Through! And then you'll be lost . . . gone forever . . ." She burst into tears.

"There, there, Sisli, don't cry," Lafayette soothed, holding her in his arms. "Things aren't all that bad. We still have a little time. Maybe I'll get the knack of it yet—or maybe he won't come after all—or—"

"I'll . . . I'll try to be brave." Sisli brushed away her tears and smiled up at Lafayette. "You're right. There's still time. We can't give up. Now try again: close your eyes, think of the wall as being woven of little lines of light. And the lines of light are only tiny specks that move very fast—so fast they aren't really there—and you reach out . . . you feel them, you match the pattern of your mind to them, and—"

"All right," Vugdo's blunt voice spoke suddenly beside them. "Wizner Hiz is waiting. Let's go, Haz."

The glowering youth stood just inside the impervious wall—impervious to O'Leary, at least, he thought disgustedly. Around here, every man, woman, and child over eighteen months had freedom to come and go—all but him!

"He's not ready," Sisli had jumped up, stood facing her brother. "Hiz will have to wait."

"You know better than that."

"Go away! You're spoiling everything! If you'd just give us more time—"

"It's not me—it's Wizner Hiz—"

"Yes, indeed it *is* Wizner Hiz," a new voice spoke, a

sharp, thin-edged voice that seemed to slice between Lafayette's bones. He turned to see a lean, leathery-faced old Wingman, with a few gray plumes still clinging to his withered scalp, a nose like an eagle's beak, eyes like bits of glowing coal.

"And I am here," Wizner Hiz said in an ominous hiss, "to discover the truth of this curious matter!"

"There's nothing to discover," Sisli spoke up defiantly, facing the Visioner. "Tazlo had a fall; he hit his head. Naturally, he was a bit confused. But now . . . he remembers everything—don't you, Tazlo?" She turned to face him, her eyes bright with fear, and with determination.

"Well—there may be a few details I haven't quite remembered yet," he temporized.

"So? That is good news indeed," Wizner snapped. "But of course the matter is not one which can be settled so casually. The interest of all Thallathlone are concerned. People are afraid of the worst. They require reassurance. I'm sure you'll willingly join with me in laying all fears at rest."

"Of course he will," Sisli spoke up quickly. "But he needs more rest. He hasn't recovered—"

"I have no intention of overstraining an honest invalid," Wizner cut in harshly. "A few questions, a few tests, publicly given—nothing more. Then honest Tazlo—if indeed the subject *is* Tazlo—can return to his sickbed—if—he is still in need of special attention."

"Tomorrow! He'll feel much better tomorrow—"

"Tomorrow may be too late, girl!"

"He might have a relapse if he has to go out now—"

"Suppose—" Wizner pointed a taloned finer at Sisli. "Suppose this man we call Tazlo Haz *is* in truth Invaded by a parasite from the dark spaces between the worlds! Would you nurture him here, assist him to prepare a place for others of his fell breed?"

"He isn't! I know he isn't!"

"Sisli—he has to be put to the test," Henbo interrupted. "Fighting it will only make it look worse for him. If he *is* Tazlo, it will all be over in a few minutes! It can't hurt to answer a few questions, even if he is still a little weak—and he looks strong enough to me," he added, giving Lafayette a look that was far from cordial.

"He'll come with you now," Vugdo stated flatly. "Won't you, Tazlo?"

Lafayette looked at the Wingman. He looked at Wizner Hiz. He looked at Sisli. He drew a breath.

"No," he said. "I'm afraid I can't oblige, fellows."

"No, you say?" the Visioner shrilled. "But I say *yes!* Vugdo—Henbo—take him!"

"Come on, you—" Vugdo caught Lafayette's arm; Henbo seized his injured wing in a secure grip, twisted as Lafayette held back. Sisli screamed. Her father made distressed sounds. Lafayette braced his feet, but the pain in the broken member was like a hot sword under his shoulder blade. They hustled him forward, slammed him against the unyielding wall with stunning force.

"What's that?" said Vugdo, who stood half in, half out of the wall, gaping at O'Leary. "Merge, man! Merge! This resistance is foolish!"

"Sorry," Lafayette said. "No can do. I seem to have forgotten how."

"Aha!" Wizner crowed. "You see? Proof! Proof positive! That was how we dealt with them last time, how we trapped them in the end! The Mind-gobblers had not our skill in merging! A wall of kreewood trapped them like weeki birds in a cage! And so we caged them, starved them—"

"No! It's not true!" Sisli wailed. "He's simply forgotten!"

"Silence, foolish chit! Would you shield the monster in our midst?"

"He's not a monster!"

"So? How can you be sure?"

"Because . . . because I've looked into his eyes—and he's good!"

"Then let him step forth—and prove himself a Wingman!"

"It's no use, Sisli," Lafayette said. "I can't, and that's that."

"Then you admit you're a Mind-gobbler!" Wizner Hiz screeched, backing away. Vugdo and Henbo retreated, staring at him. Only Sisli still clung to his arm, until her father dragged her away.

"No," Lafayette said. "I don't admit anything of the sort."

"Come, let him prove himself," Wizner Hiz snarled. "We'll withdraw and leave him to himself. If he's a true man and not possessed, he'll emerge. If not—then let him be sealed up forever as a warning to others of his dread kind!"

In silence, except for Sisli's sobbing, Sisli's father and brothers trooped out through the wall as through a veil of dark-brown smoke. Wizner Hiz took the girl's arm, dragged her with him, still protesting.

Lafayette was alone in the sealed room.

4

There was a little of the fruit juice left in the cups; O'Leary drank half, preserving the rest for later. He circled the room, vainly prodding and poking in search of some overlooked egress.

"Don't waste your time," he advised himself, slumping on the bed. "There's no way out—except through the wall. You're trapped. You've had it. This is where it all ends . . . trapped by a silly superstition . . ."

"But," his thoughts ran on, "maybe it's not a superstition at that. In a way Wizner's right: I *am* an Invader. Apparently, this fellow Tazlo Haz is a real person—at least as real as any of this world. I haven't simply sprouted wings—I've taken over someone else's body. And it was the same when I was Zorro!" He rose, pacing the cell.

"Zorro really existed; he was a Wayfarer, with a girlfriend named Gizelle, and a big career ahead as a pickpocket. Until I came along and swiped his identity. And then . . ." O'Leary paused, rubbing his chin thoughtfully. "Then I switched identities again—with Tazlo Haz. And this time, I switched worlds along with bodies. Why not? I've done it before, more than once. The USA—Artesia—then half a dozen continua that Goruble dumped me into when he was trying to get rid of me—then Melange. And now Thallathlone."

He sat on the bed again. "But why? At first I thought it was the Focal Referent. I pushed the button, and the next thing I knew no one recognized me. But this time I didn't have the Mark III. I was just standing there. And another thing: always before the parallel worlds I've stumbled into had the same geography as Colby Corners. There were a few variables—such as the desert in Artesia where the bay was back home—but that was relatively minor. But here—nothing's the same. It's a totally different setup, with a valley where the mountain was. And the people aren't analogs of the ones I knew—like Swinehild being Adoranne's double, and Hulk, Count Alain's. . . ."

He rose again, paced restlessly. "I have to make a few assumptions: one, that I really did get a note from the Red Bull, I really did meet him at the A & D, and that somehow I changed places with Zorro—" He stopped dead. "Which implies . . . that Zorro changed places with *me!*"

5

"Oh, boy," Lafayette was still muttering half an hour later. "This changes everything. Nobody will be out looking for me. Or if they do, they'll find me wandering in a dazed condition, claiming I'm somebody named Zorro the Pig. Or they've already found me. I'm probably back home now, with Daphne fussing over me, feeding me soup. Or feeding Zorro soup!" He threw himself down on the bunk. "Just wait till I get my hands on that slimy character! Posing as me, insinuating himself into Daphne's good graces . . ." He paused while a startled expression fixed itself on his face. "Why, that dirty, underhanded, sneaking louse! Taking advantage of poor Daphne that way! I've got to get out of here! I have to get home!" He sprang up, hammered on the wall, shouted.

The silence was total. Lafayette slumped against the wall. "Great," he muttered. "Pound some more. Yell a lot. All that will do is convince Wizner Hiz you're just what he claims—if anyone can hear you, which is doubtful. That wood's as hard as armor plate." He sat on the bed, rubbing his bruised fists. "And he's probably right. Thallathlone is obviously some kind of offbeat plane of existence, not a regular parallel continuum. Maybe it's on some kind of diagonal with the serial universes Central controls. Maybe people like me have accidentally wound up here before, just the way I did; maybe there's some kind of probability fault line you can slip through. . . ."

He lay back with a sigh. The ray of sunlight from above made a bright spot on the dark, polished floor. The perfume of Sisli still lingered in the air.

"Maybe a lot of things," he murmured. "Maybe I'd better get some sleep. Maybe I'll be able to think better then. . . ."

6

The dream was a pleasant one: he was lying on the bank of a river, under the spreading branches of a sycamore, with Daphne beside him, murmuring to him in a soft and loving voice.

. . . *try, please for me . . . you can do it, I know you can do it . . .*

"Try what?" Lafayette said genially, and moved to put his arm about her shoulders. But somehow she was gone now; he was alone under the tree . . . and the light had faded. He was in darkness, still hearing her call, faint, as from a great distance:

. . . . *just for me, my Tazlo . . . please try . . . please . . .*

"Daphne? Where are you?" He rose, groping in the pitch darkness. "Where did you go?"

*Come to me . . . come . . . you can if you try . . . try . . . try . . . try . . .*

"Certainly—but where are you? Daphne?"

*Try, Tazlo! You are trying! I can feel you trying! Like this! You see? Hold your mind this way . . . and move like this . . .*

He felt ephemeral hands touch his mind. He felt the latticework of thought turned gently, aligned, steered. There was a gentle tugging, as if a cotton thread pulled at him. He moved forward, listening, listening to her voice. Cobwebs brushed his face, dragged back over his body, *through* his body. . . .

Cool, fresh air around him, filled with a soft, rustling sound. He smelled green, growing things; he opened his eyes, saw the twinkle of stars through the filigree of foliage above, saw lights that gleamed through leaves, saw—

"Sisli!" he blurted. "How . . . what—"

She was in his arms. "Tazlo—my Tazlo—I knew you could do it! I knew!"

He turned, looked at the corrugated surface of shaggy bark behind him. He ran his hand over it, feeling the solidity of it, the denseness.

"Well, what do you know," he said wonderingly. "I walked through a wall."

# CHAPTER SIX

## 1

Wizner Hiz was still scowling; but even Vugdo had taken Sisli's side—and Lafayette's.

"You told us the fact that the wall stopped him proved he'd been Invaded," the Wingman said. "But sure enough, after he had a little time to get it together, out he came— just as Sisli said he would."

"You were the one that set up the test, Wizner Hiz," Henbo shrugged. "Don't complain when he passes it."

"Come along, Tazlo," Sisli said with a toss of her head. "The party is about to begin."

Lafayette hesitated, looking out along the yard-thick branch with the shiny path worn along its upper surface, leading toward the lighted dancing pavillion. "What happens," he inquired, "if you slip?"

"Why should you slip?" Sisli walked out a few feet, stood on one toe and pirouetted, spreading her white wings just enough to make a sighing sound and stir the leaves around her.

"I've got a broken wing, remember?" O'Leary improvised. "I've got an idea: why don't we stay here, and just sort of listen in from a distance."

"Silly boy." She caught his hand, led him out on the precarious path. "Just close your eyes and I'll lead you," she said with an impish smile. "I think you just want to be babied," she added.

"Let's go," Vugdo said, jostling past Lafayette, almost sending him from the branch. "I have some drinking to catch up on, after the day I've been through."

O'Leary clung to a cluster of leaves he had grabbed for support; Sisli pulled him back.

"For heaven's sake, Tazlo—stop behaving as if you weren't one of Thallathlone's top athletes. You're embarrassing me."

"Sure; just give me time to get my sky-legs." He closed his eyes and concentrated. "It's funny, Sisli," he said, "but if I just relax and sort of clear my mind—fit myself into the Tazlo bag—I start remembering things. Little bits and pieces, like, oh, sailing through the air on a sunny day—and doing power dives over Yawning Abyss—and even walking branches . . ."

"Well, of course, Tazlo; you've done them often enough."

"And . . . even with my eyes closed, I can feel you, standing there, six feet away. I can sense Vugdo, he's about thirty feet away now, talking to someone. And I think Henbo has gone back . . . in that direction." He pointed.

"Well, of course we can sense each other," Sisli sounded puzzled. "How else would we manage to find our way back to the eyrie after a long flight?"

"I guess it figures. And all I have to do to walk these branches is just hold my mind right, right?"

"Right." Sisli giggled. "You look so solemn and determined, as if you were going to have to do something terribly brave and terribly important—all just to take a stroll down the front walk."

"All things are relative, I guess," Lafayette said, and stepped boldly out behind her toward the sounds of music.

Life in Thallathlone was pretty nice, all things considered, O'Leary reflected hazily, relaxing at the nightly fete. If it wasn't one occasion for joy, it was another. Tonight's ball, for example, had been in celebration of the second week's anniversary of his vindication. The fermented booljuice had flowed freely; the air dancers had been skilled and graceful in their wispy scarves and veils, the toasted birdseed had tasted better than broiled steak—and Sisli, at his side every minute, had been as loving and attentive a prospective bride as a man could want.

That was the only thought that dampened his enthusiasm momentarily.

"But actually, everything will turn out fine," he reminded himself for the tenth time. "As soon as I figure out how to get back into my own body, Tazlo Haz will be back in his. He may have a pretty wild story to tell, but it can all be blamed on the bump on my head. And he and Sisli will live happily ever after."

*Swell,* he answered himself. *Just as long as you don't get carried away and spend the wedding night with the bride.*

"Which reminds me—that feathered four-flusher is probably romancing Daphne right now!"

*Nor any more than you're romancing Sisli.*

"You mean he's kissed her?"

*Wouldn't you?*

"Certainly—but that's different. When I kiss Sisli, it's just . . . just friendly."

*So is he. You can count on that.*

"I'll break his other wing, that bird in wolf's clothing!"

*Not until he's back inside the birdskin, I hope.*

"Tazlo—who are you talking to?" Sisli inquired.

"Ah—just a fellow named O'Leary. A sort of figment of my imagination. Or maybe I'm a figment of his. It's a question for the philosophers."

"Isn't that who you said you were when you were still delirious?"

"I may have mentioned the name. But I'm much better now, right?" He blinked away the double images and focused a smile on the girl's inquiring face. "After all—I *did* merge—and I walked the branches—and ate bird-seed—and—"

"Tazlo—you frighten me when you talk like this. It's as though—as though you were playing a role instead of just being yourself."

"Think nothing of it, m'dear," Lafayette said solemnly. "You're letting what old Wizzy said bug you. Lot of nonsense. Mind-grabbers indeed. Probably just some poor Central agent with a short circuit in his probability wiring, meaning no harm at all."

"Harmless, eh?" an unfriendly voice snapped from near at hand. Wizner Hiz glowered from his perch a few feet above and to one side of the tiny table where Lafayette sat with Sisli. "I've been watching you, Haz—or whoever you are. You don't behave normally. You don't feel right—"

"Of course he's still a little strange," Sisli burst out. "He hasn't fully recovered from the blow on his head!"

"Go away, Wiggy Hig," Lafayette called carelessly. "Or Higgly Wig. Your sour pus bothers me. The night was made for love. Especially tonight, up here in a treetop. Back home they'll never believe all this . . ." He waved a hand to include the paper lanterns strung in the branches, the gaily dressed wingmen and women fluttering gaily about, the high moon riding above.

"Back home? And where might that be?" the Visioner said sharply.

"It's just a figure of speech," Sisli said quickly. "Leave him alone, Wizner Hiz! He's not hurting anyone!"

"Neither did the others—at first. Then they started . . . changing. You don't remember, girl; you were too young. But I saw it! I saw Boolbo Biz start turning into a monster before our eyes!"

"Well, Tazlo's not turning into a monster," Sisli said, and took his arm possessively.

"Course not," Lafayette said, and wagged a finger at the old Wingman. "Just the same old me—whoever that is.

Get lost, Wiz—I mean Hiz—" He paused as something fluttered past his face. Twisting on his wicker stool, he saw a large, russet feather drifting down through the foliage below.

"Someone shedding?" he asked genially. A second feather followed the first. Something touched his arm: a third feather. He made brushing motions. "What's going on here?" he inquired as more feathers swirled around him. He stood, caught sight of Sisli's horror-stricken expression.

"Wha's . . . what's the matter?" he asked, and blew a downy feather from his upper lip.

"Oh, no—Tazlo, no!" Sisli yelped.

"Aha!" Wizner Hiz screeched.

"Grab him!" Vugdo bellowed.

"Grab who?" Lafayette demanded, looking around for the victim. His question was answered as hands caught at him, clamped on his arms, dragged him to the center of the dancing pavilion, amid a cloud of feathers.

"What's this all about?" he yelled. "I've passed your test, haven't I . . ." His voice trailed away as he caught sight of his unbroken wing, held in the grasp of half a dozen wide-eyed Thallathlonians. Even as he stared, another handful of feathers came free to swirl away in a sudden gust of wind.

"Not quite, Mind-grabber," Wizner Hiz rasped. "Not quite!"


3


Four sturdily muscled Wingmen with stout ten-foot poles prodded at Lafayette, keeping him immobilized at the center of the cleared open-work pavilion. All around, the ranked population of the eyrie clustered in a circle, ten deep, all eyes on him. Sisli was gone, borne away weeping by her brothers. So far as O'Leary could tell, there was not a friendly expression in sight.

"Don't do anything hasty," he urged as a pole-tip poked him painfully in the ribs. "I can't fly, remember? I know it looks bad, but I'll think of an explanation if you'll just—*ooof!*" His appeal was cut short by a hearty jab to the abdomen.

"Never fear, we know how to deal with your kind," Wizner Hiz crowed. He rubbed his hands together, skipping about beyond the pole-wielders with the agility of a ten-year-old, shaping up the crowd.

"You there—back a few feet! Hold it! Now you, ladies —just move in here, fill up this gap. You—the tall one —move back! Now, Pivlo Poo, you and Quigli step in here . . . close it up . . ."

"This looks like . . . a public execution," O'Leary pushed the words out painfully. "I hope you're not planning anything so barbaric—"

"All together, now," Wizner Hiz commanded, raising his hands for silence. He whistled a shrill note—like a pitch pipe—and gestured. An answering note came from the massed voices of the eyrie.

"Choir practice? At a time like this!" Lafayette wondered aloud.

"It will be the last choir you'll hear in this world," Wizner Hiz shrilled, fixing Lafayette with a beady eye filled with triumph. "You're about to be Sung Out! Out of the world! Back to the dark spaces you came from, foul Invader!"

"Oh, really?" Lafayette smiled painfully. "What happens if I fail to disappear? Does that prove I'm innocent?"

"Never fear—the Chant of Exorcism has never failed," one of the strong-arm men assured him. "But if it does—we'll think of something else."

"Actually, it's just a simple case of falling feathers, fellows," Lafayette said. "I could happen to anyone—"

At a sweeping gesture from Wizner Hiz, a chorus of sound burst from the choir, drowning Lafayette's appeal.

88

Out of the world
　Away and beyond
Back through the veil
　Stranger begone
Afloat on a sea
　Wider than night
Deeper and deeper
　Sinking from sight
Back where you came from
　Grabber of souls
Back to the depths
　Where the great bell tolls
Out of the world
Far from the sun
Of fair Thallathlone
　Forever begone
Borne on the wings
　Of the magic song
Forever begone
　From fair Thallathlone. . . .

The chant went on and on, waves of sound that waxed and waned, rolling at Lafayette from all sides, beating at him like the waves of the sea. There was a tune: an eerie, groaning, melody repeated over and over.

. . . *Out of the world*
　*Away and beyond*. . .
*Forever begone*
　*From fair Thallathlone*. . . .

The mouths of the singers seemed to move silently, like fish gaping in water, while the moaning chant, independent of them, rose and fell, rose and fell. The faces were blurring, running together.

. . . *Far and away* . . .
　*Stranger begone* . . .
*Forever begone*
　*From Fair Thallathlone* . . .

The words seemed to come from a remote distance now. The lights had faded and winked out; O'Leary could no longer see the faces of the singers, could no longer feel the wicker floor under his feet. Only the song remained—a palpable force that enfolded him, lifted him, floated him away into lightless depths, then faded, dwindled, became a ghostly echo fading in utter darkness, utter emptiness.

## 4

Lafayette stared into the inky blackness, making vague swimming motions. Something that glowed fanitly appeared in the distance, sailed closer in a great spiral, goggled at him with yard-wide eyes, spiraled off into the darkness.

"Which way is up?" O'Leary inquired; but there was no sound. In fact, he realized there was no mouth, no tongue, no lungs.

"*Good lord! I'm not breathing. . .* The thought seemed to jump forth and hang in space, glowing like a neon sign. Other bits and pieces of mind-stuff came swirling around him, like flotsam in a millrace:

*. . . oother-boober of the umber-wumber . . .*

*. . . try a section ooty-toot, or maybe a number tot noodle . . .*

*. . . told him to drop dead, the louse . . .*

*. . . eemie-weemie-squeemie-pip-pip . . .*

*. . . so I says to him . . .*

*. . . to the right, hold it, hold it . . . don't move . . .*

*. . . HEY—I GOT A ROGUE BOGIE ON NUMBER TWELVE!*

*. . . smarmy parmy, whiffly niffly, weeky squeeky . . .*

*. . . aw, come on, baby . . .*

*. . . HEY—YOU—IDENTIFY!*

*. . . poom-poom-poom . . .*

*. . . so I ups to him and he ups to me and I ups to him . . .*

. . . HELLO, NARK NINE. I'VE GOT A SPOOK READING IN NUMBER TWELVE STAGING AREA.

UH-HUH. I READ IT. JUST GARBAGE, DUMP IT, BARF ONE.

NIX—I PICKED UP A BEEP ON OH SIX OH, NARK NINE. COULD BE A ROGUE.

. . . NIK-NIK-NIK . . .

DUMP IT, BARF ONE. WE GOT TRAFFIC TO HANDLE, REMEMBER?

HEY— YOU! GIVE ME A BEEP ON SIX OH OR I DUMP, YOU READ?

Something that resembled a tangle of glowing coat-hanger wire sailed purposefully up to O'Leary, hovered before him, rotating slowly.

"It looks like a disembodied migraine," he said. "I wonder if it would go away if I closed my eyes . . . if I had any eyes to close."

OK, THAT'S BETTER. NOW LET'S HAVE THAT SNAG NUMBER.

"Since I don't have eyes, obviously I'm not actually seeing things," Lafayette advised himself. "Still, some kind of impressions are impinging on me—and my brain is interpreting them as sight and sound. But—"

ANSWER ME, BUSTER!

"Who," Lafayette said. "Me?"

FLIPPIN A! SNAG NUMBER, PRONTO. YOU GOT TRAFFIC BACKED UP SIX HEXAMETERS ON NINE LEVELS!

"Who are you? Where are you? Where am I? Get me out of here!" Lafayette blurted, twisting to look all around him.

SURE—AS SOON AS YOU GIVE ME A SNAG NUMBER TO LATCH ONTO!

"I don't know what a snag number is! It looks as if I'm floating in some sort of luminous alphabet soup. Not the soup, the alphabet, you understand—"

A man came tumbling slowly out of the darkness

toward Lafayette, end over end. He was dressed in what appeared to be a sequinned leotard, and he glowed with a greenish light; Lafayette leaped toward him with a glad cry. Too fast; he braced himself for the collision, caught a glimpse of a startled face twisting to stare at him in the instant before contact.

There was no impact; only a sense of diving into a cloud of whirling particles, tugged at by surging forces—

*What in the name of two dozen dancing devils on a bass drum!* a strange voice roared.

Light and sound burst upon O'Leary. He was staring at a plastic plate attached to his wrist, with the stamped legend:

SNAG NUMBER 1705

*LAST CHANCE, BUSTER! GOING . . . GOING . . .*

"Snag number one thousand seven hundred and five!" O'Leary yelled.

From somewhere, a giant, unseen hook came, caught him by the back of the neck, and threw him across the Universe.

5

When Lafayette's head stopped whirling, he was standing in a chamber no bigger than an elevator, with opalescent, softly glowing walls, ceiling, and floor. A red light blinked on one wall; there was a soft *snick*!; the panel facing him opened like a revolving door on a large, pale-green room with a carpeted floor, a sound-absorbent ceiling, and a desk behind which sat an immaculately groomed woman of indeterminate age, extremely good looking in spite of pale green hair and a total lack of eyebrows. She gave him a crisp look, waved to a chair, poked a button on her desk.

"Rough one?" she asked in a tone of businesslike sympathy.

"Ah . . . just average," Lafayette said cautiously, looking around the room, which was furnished with easy chairs, potted palsm, sporting prints, and softly murmuring air-conditioner grills.

"You want a stretcher, or can you make it under your own power?" the green-haired receptionist inquired briskly as Lafayette edged into the room.

"What? Oh, I suppose you mean my bandaged wing. Actually it doesn't bother me all that much, thanks."

The woman frowned. "Psycho damage?"

"Well—frankly, I'm a little confused. I know it must sound silly, but . . . who are you? Where am I?"

"Oh, brother." The woman poked another button, spoke toward an unseen intercom. "Frink, get a trog team up here; and a stretcher. I've got a 984 for you, and it looks like a doozie." She gave Lafayette a look of weary sympathy. "Might as well sit down and take it easy, fellow." She wagged her head like one subjected to trials above and beyond the call of Job Description.

"Thanks." O'Leary sat gingerly on the edge of a low, olive-leather chair. "You, uh, know me?" he inquired.

The woman spread her hands in a noncommittal gesture. "How can I keep track of over twelve hundred ops?" She blinked as if an idea had just occurred to her. "You're not amnac?"

"Who's he?"

"Mama mia. Amnac means no memory. Loss of identity. In other words, you don't remember your own name."

"Frankly, there does seem to be a little uncertainty about that."

"Right hand, index finger," she said wearily. Lafayette approached the desk and offered the digit, which the woman grasped and pressed against a glass plate set in the desk top, one of an array of similar plates interspersed with countersunk buttons. A light winked, fluttered, blinked off. Letters appeared on a ground-glass screen in front of the receptionist.

"Raunchini," she said. "Dink 9, Franchet 43, undercategory Gimmel. Ring a bell?" She looked at him hopefully.

"Not deafeningly," Lafayette temporized. "Look here,

ma'am—I may as well be frank with you. I seen to have stumbled into something that's over my head—"

"Hold it, Raunchini. You can cover all that in your debriefing. I'm strictly admin myself."

"You don't understand. The fact is, I don't know what's going on. I mean, I started off in perfect innocence to have a drink with an old associate, and when I saw what he'd stumbled on, I realized right away that it was a matter for—for higher authorities to handle. But . . ." he looked around the room. "I have a distinct feeling I'm not in Artesia; there's nothing like this there. So the question naturally occurs—where am I?"

"You're at Central Casting, naturally. Look, just take a chair over there, and—"

"Central? I thought so! Thank Groot! Then all my problems are solved!" Lafayette sank down gratefully on the corner of the desk. "Look, I have some vital data to transmit to the proper quarter. I've discovered that when Goruble defected, he stashed away a whole armory of stolen gear—"

A door across the room swung open and a pair of husky young men in crisp, pale-blue hospital garb stepped into the room, guiding between them a flat, six-foot slab of what looked like foam rubber. The latter floated without support two feet above the floor, bobbing slightly like an air mattress on water.

"OK, fella," one of them said, unlimbering a large and complicated-looking hyperdermic, "we'll have you comfy in two and a half demisecs. Just hop up here and stretch out, facedown—"

"I don't need a stretcher," Lafayette snapped. "I need someone to listen to what I have to say."

"Sure, you'll get your chance, fella," the orderly said soothingly, advancing. "Simmer down—"

Lafayette scrambled around behind the desk. "Listen—get Nicodaeus! He knows me! What I've got to report is triple X-UTS priority! I demand a hearing, or heads will be rolling around here like spilled marbles!"

The orderly looked uncertain, glanced at the woman for support. She waved her hands helplessly. "Don't look at me," she said. "I'm just the flunky on the front desk. Stand by one; Belarius is Duty Officer; I'll get him up here and let him stick his neck out." She pushed buttons and spoke briefly. The orderly flipped a switch at the head of the stretcher; it sank to the floor.

Three minutes passed in a tense silence, with Lafayette hovering behind the desk, the stretcher-bearers yawning and scratching, and the green-haired woman furiously filing her iridescent-green nails. Then a tall, wide-shouldered man with smooth gray hair and a professorial air strode into the room. He glanced around, pursed his lips at Lafayette.

"Well, Miss Dorch?" he said in a mellow baritone.

"This is Agent Raunchini, sir. He's apparently a 984 case; but he won't accept sedation—"

"I'm not Agent Raunchini," Lafayette snapped. "And I have priority information to report!"

"A contradiction in terms, eh?" The newcomer gave Lafayette a glassy smile. "Just go along, there's a good fellow—"

"I want to talk to Inspector Nicodaeus!"

"Impossible. He's on a field assignment, won't be back for six months."

"I'll make a deal," O'Leary said. "Listen to what I have to say, and then I'll go quietly, fair enough? Spurd knows I could use a nap." He yawned.

Belarius looked at his wristwatch. "Young man, I don't lightly upset the routine of this Center—"

"What about a Focal Referent in unauthorized hands?" Lafayette cut in. "Is that worth missing a coffee break for?"

Belarius' urbane expression drained away.

"Did you say—don't say it!" He held up a well-manicured hand, shot a nervous glance at the others in the room.

"Possibly I'd best have a chat with Agent Raunchini after all," he said. "A private chat. Suppose we go along to my office, eh?" He gave Lafayette a smile like a warning blinker and turned to the door.

"Well, now we're getting somewhere," Lafayette murmured as he followed.

6

The gray-haired man led Lafayette along a silent corridor to a small room, unadorned except for a row of framed photographs of determined faces lining the walls. Belarius seated himself behind an impressive bleached oak desk, gestured Lafayette to a chair.

"Now, just make a clean breast of the whole matter," he said in a sternly avuncular tone. "And I'll undertake to put in a word for you."

"Sure, fine," Lafayette hitched his chair closer. "It was a Mark III. And according to—to a reliable source, there's more where that came from. With luck, he won't have had time to cart all the stuff into town and sell it—"

"Kindly begin at the beginning, Agent. When were you first approached?"

"Two weeks ago. I found the note rolled up in a pair of socks, and—"

"Who was your contact?"

"Let's leave his name out of it; he didn't know what he was getting into. As I was saying, the note told me to meet him—"

"The name, Raunchini. Don't attempt to shield your confederates!"

"Will you let me get on with it? And my name's not Raunchini!"

"Now you're claiming to be a prep, eh? That would imply a conspiracy of considerable scope. What do you allege to have done with the real Raunchini?"

"Nothing! Stop changing the subject! The important

thing is to grab the loot before the Red Bu—before anyone else gets their hands on it—and to recover the Mark III!"

"Mark II. You may leave that aspect of the matter to me. I want names, dates, drop points, amounts paid—"

"You're all mixed up," Lafayette cut in. "I don't know a thing about all that. All I know is the Mark III was stolen from me while I was asleep, and—" He paused, looking at one of the photos, showing an elderly gentleman with a vague smile and a pince-nez.

"How? With a derrick?" Belarius asked querulously.

"What? How do I know? I had it in my secret pocket, and—"

"Pocket! Look here, Raunchini—don't attempt to make a fool of me! Your only hope for clemency is strict veracity and total recall!"

"My name's not Raunchini!"

Belarius glared, then turned to a small console at his elbow and jabbed at a button.

"Full dossier on Agent Raunchini," he ordered. "And double-check the ID."

"Look here, Mr. Belarius," Lafayette said. "you can play with your buttons later. Right now you need to get a squad in there to collect the stuff and find that Mark III before Lom uses it!"

Belarius turned as the panel behind him *beep!*ed.

"Definite confirmation of Raunchini ID," a crisp voice said.

"Retinal and palm prints check out too. Junior Field Agent, assigned to Locus Beta Two-Four, Plane P-122; Charlie 381-f."

"Your wires are crossed," Lafayette said. "I'm Lafayette O'Leary—or I used to be. Right now I'm Tazlo Haz—"

"Stop babbling, man! An insanity plea won't help you!"

"Who's insane? Why don't you listen to me? I'm trying to save your bacon for you!"

"I doubt if you've ever seen a Focal Referent," Belarius snapped. "You obviously haven't the faintest notion of the machine's physical characteristics."

"Oh, no? It's about six inches high, with a plastic case with a bunch of wires and wheels inside!"

"That does it," Belarius said flatly. "The Mark II is a great improvement over earlier models; but it still weighs four and a half tons, and occupies three cubic yards of space!"

"Oh, yeah?" O'Leary came back. "You obviously don't know what you're talking about!"

"I happen," Belarius rasped, "to be Chief of Research and Project Officer for the Focal Referent program—which happens to be classified *Unthinkable Secret!*"

"Well—I'm thinking about it—"

With a quick motion, Belarius lifted what was obviously a hand weapon from beneath the desk.

"Send a squad of enforcers to Trog 87 on the double," he said over his shoulder to the intercom.

"Just a minute," Lafayette protested. "You're making a big mistake! I admit it looks a little strange, my having wings—"

"Wings?" Belarius edged backward in his chair. "Hurry up with that enforcer squad," he said over his shoulder. "He may get violent at any moment and I'd dislike to be forced to vaporize him before we get to the bottom of this."

"I can explain," Lafayette insisted. "Or—well, I can't explain it, but I can assure you it's all perfectly normal, in an abnormal sort of way."

"Never mind the protestations," Belarius said grimly. "Sane or otherwise, I'll soon have the truth out of you via brain-scrape. It may leave your cerebrum a trifle soggy, but in matters of Continuum security, there's no room for half measures!"

"Why don't you check my story out?" Lafayette protested. "What makes you so sure you know it all?"

"If there were one hard datum to check, Raunchini, I'd gladly do so!"

"Listen," O'Leary said desperately, "check on me:
98

O'Leary; Lafayette O'Leary, part-time agent for Artesia!"

Belarius pushed out his lips, gave a curt order to the Intercom. As they waited, Lafayette's eyes strayed back to the photo which had caught his eye. He had seen that face somewhere . . .

"Who's he?" he asked, pointing.

Belarius raised an eyebrow, following O'Leary's pointing finger. His expression flickered.

"Why do you ask?" he inquired casually.

"I've seen him—somewhere. Recently."

"Where?" Belarius came back crisply.

Lafayette shook his head. "I don't remember. All those blows on the head—"

"So—you're going to play it cagy, eh?" Belarius snarled. "What's your price for selling out? Immunity? Cash? Relocation?"

"I don't know what you're talking about," O'Leary snapped. "I just—"

"All right, you've got me over a barrel! You know how badly we want to get our hands on Jorlemagne! I won't hassle! Immunity, a million in cash, and the Locus of your choice. Is it a deal?"

O'Leary frowned in puzzlement. "Maybe you've been wearing tight hats," he said. "You don't seem to grasp the idea—"

"Raunchini—I'll have the full story out of you if it's the last thing I do!"

"O'Leary!" Lafayette matched the other's shout.

"O'Leary. Got it right here, Chief," the intercom blatted suddenly.

"Well, thank heaven," Lafayette sighed.

"Would that be Lorenzo, Lafcadio, Lothario, Lancelot, Leopold, or Ludwig?" the voice came back, businesslike.

"Lafayette," he supplied.

"Uh-huh. Here it is. Reserve appointment to classified Locus. Inactive."

"Physical description?" Belarius snapped.

"Six feet, one-seventy, light-brown hair, blue eyes, harmless appearance—"

99

"Hey," Lafayette protested.

Belarius swiveled to face him. "Ready to come clean now?"

"Look, I can explain," Lafayette said, feeling the sweat start on his forehead. "You see, I accidentally activated the Focal Referent. It was unintentional, you understand—"

"And—"

"And—well, I . . . I changed shape! Apparently I turned into this Tazlo Haz person, and—"

"You were transformed from O'Leary into Haz, is that it?" Belarius said wearily, passing a hand over his face. "Your story grows steadily more remarkable."

"Not exactly," Lafayette demurred. "Before I was Haz I was a fellow named Zorro."

Belarius sighed. "Doesn't this sound a trifle idiotic—even to your fevered brain?"

"All right! I can't help how it sounds; what matters is that there's a truckload of stolen Probability Lab gear lying there in the cave waiting for anybody who happens along, and—"

"And where might this alleged cave be located?"

"In Artesia—just outside the city of the same name!"

"Never heard of it." Belarius turned and snapped a question at the intercom, glared at O'Leary as he waited for an answer.

"Right, chief," the voice at the other end came back. "Here it is: Plane V-87, Fox 22 1-b, Alpha Nine-three."

"Are we carrying out any operations there?"

"No, sir. We closed the file out last year."

There was a short pause. "Well, I'll be graunched, sir. The classified Locus this Agent O'Leary was assigned to checks out as this same V-87, Fox 22 1-b, Alpha Nine-three. I'll have to post that to the file—" the voice broke off. "Odd, sir—it seems we have a new recruit on the roster, from the Locus in question, just arrived yesterday."

"Name?"

"O'Leary. Say, that's funny; O'Leary is coded inactive in the main bank—"

"You say O'Leary is here at Central Casting—now?"

"Affirmative, sir."

"Send O'Leary up to Trog 87 immediately." Belarius frowned bleakly at Lafayette. "We'll get to the bottom of this matter," he muttered.

"I don't get it," Lafayette said. "I'm down in your records as having arrived here yesterday?"

"Not you, Raunchini: O'Leary." Belarius drummed on the desk. There was a brief buzz from the door and four uniformed men entered with drawn handguns.

"Stand by, men," Belarius ordered, waving them back.

"I'll bet it's Lorenzo," Lafayette said. "Or possibly Lothario. But how could they have gotten to Artesia? They belong in completely different loci . . ."

A harassed-looking junior official entered, turned to usher in a second new arrival—a small, trim, feminine figure, neatly dressed in a plain white tunic and white knee-boots; she scanned the room with immense, dark eyes, a slight, anxious smile on her delicately modeled lips.

"Good lord," Lafayette blurted, jumping to his feet. "Daphne!"

# CHAPTER SEVEN

## 1

For a moment there was total silence. Belarius looked from Lafayette to the girl and back again. She stared at Lafayette; he grinned a vast and foolish grin and started toward her.

"How in the world did you get here, girl? When they told me they had an O'Leary here, it never occurred to me it might be——"

"How do you know my name?" Daphne cut in with surprising sharpness. She spun to face Belarius. "Who is this man? Does he know anything about Lafayette?"

"Do I know anything about Lafayette?" O'Leary cried. "Daphne, I guess the wings fooled you. Don't you know me?"

"I never saw you before in my life! What have you done to my husband?"

"I haven't done anything to your husband! I *am* your husband!"

"Stay away from me!" She took refuge behind a large cop, who put a protective arm around her shoulders.

"Get your greasy paws off her, you flatfoot!" Lafayette yelled.

"One moment!" Belarius thundered. "You, Raunchini! Stand where you are! You, Recruit O'Leary: for the record: do you know this Agent?"

"I never saw him before in my life!"

"Why waste time and breath, Raunchini?" Belarius grated. "You heard O'Leary's description: six feet, one-seventy, blue eyes. You're five-five, two-ten, black eyes, swarthy complected."

"I know I'm—huh?" O'Leary paused, looked over his left shoulder, then his right. "The wings!" he blurted. "They're gone!" He looked down at himself, saw a barrel chest, generous paunch, bandy legs, pudgy-fingered hands with a dense growth of black hair on their backs. He stepped to one of the framed photos, stared at his face reflected in the glass. It was round, olive-skinned, with a flat nose and a wide mouth crowded with crooked teeth.

"Ye gods—it's happened again!" he groaned. "No wonder you thought I was crazy, talking about my wings!"

"May I go now?" Recruit O'Leary requested.

"Daphne!" Lafayette yelled. "Surely *you* know me, no matter what I look like!"

Daphne looked puzzled.

"There was this note," Lafayette went on in tones of desperation. "It was from the Red Bull; he wanted me to meet him at the A & D Tavern. I went down there, and he had this gimmick—something that Goruble had stashed in a cave. Anyway, I was looking at it, and my finger slipped, and *whap!* I turned into somebody else!"

"Is he . . . is he—" Daphne looked questioningly at Belarius, circling a shell-like ear with a slim forefinger.

"No, I'm not nuts! I tried to get back to the palace to report what I'd discovered, and the City Guard grabbed me! And before I could explain matters, Luppo and a mob of Wayfarers butted in and carted me off to their camp, but Gizelle helped me get away, and—"

"Gizelle?" Daphne pounced with unerring feminine instinct.

"Yes, uh, a fine girl, you'll love her. Anyway, she took me to her wagon, and—"

"Hmmph!" Daphne sniffed, turning away. "I'm really not interested in this person's *amours*, whoever he is!"

"It wasn't like that! It was purely platonic."

"That's enough, Raunchini!" Belarius bellowed. "O'Leary, you can go. Men, take Raunchini down to Trog Twelve and prep him for brain-scrape!"

"What's . . . what's brain-scrape?" Daphne paused at the door, casting a hesitant look at Lafayette.

"A technique for getting at the truth," Belarius growled. "Something like peeling a grape."

"Will it . . . hurt him?"

"Eh? Well, it will more or less spoil him for future use. Leaves the subject a babbling idiot in stubborn cases. But don't concern yourself, O'Leary; he'll receive his full pension, never fear."

"Daphne!" Lafayette called after her. "If you have any influence with this bunch of maniacs, tell them to listen to me!" Belarius gestured; two men stepped forward, seized Lafayette's arms, helped him toward the door.

"Tough luck, pal," one of the cops said. "I'd act nuts too, if I thought it'd get me next to a dish like that."

"I'll say," another of the escort agreed. "Brother, you don't see it stacked up like that every day—"

"That's enough out of you, Buster!" Lafayette roared, and delivered a solid kick to the shin of the luckless girl-watcher. As the man stumbled back with a yell, Lafayette jerked free, ducked under a grab, and leaped for the door. Belarius rounded his desk in time to receive a straight-arm to the mouth. O'Leary sidestepped a tackle, plunged into the corridor.

"Daphne!" O'Leary shouted as she turned and stared, wide-eyed. "If I never see you again—remember I love you! And don't forget to feed Dinny!"

"Hey—grab him!" One of the waiting stretcher-bearers yelled. Lafayette ducked aside from his reach, thrust out a foot, sending the fellow sprawling. Two more men erupted from the room. More men were advancing at a run, closing in from both directions.

"The stretcher!" Daphne cried suddenly. "Use the stretcher!"

Lafayette ducked a wild swing, sprang aboard the slab

104

hovering a foot above the carpet, jabbed the red button marked LEFT. The cot shot ceilingward, slammed him hard against the flowered wallpaper. He groped, pushed a stud at random. The stretcher shot backward, raking Lafayette across a rank of fluorescent lights. He fumbled again, dropped the cot to head height and shot forward in time to clip an oncoming security man full in the mouth, sending him bounding back against his partner. Full tilt, the cot rushed along the passage; Lafayette closed his eyes and hung on as it hurtled toward the intersection; at the last possible instant it banked, whipped around the turn, and shot at high speed through a pair of double doors—fortunately open.

The runaway steed made three swift circuits of the large green-walled room before Lafayette found a control that brought it to a shuddering halt, sending him tumbling to the rug. He rolled to hands and knees, saw that he was in the room where he had first arrived. The green-haired woman behind the desk was stabbing hysterically at her console, yelping for help.

"Here, I'll help you," Lafayette said. He scrambled up, jumped on the desk, and pushed two palmfuls of buttons, jabbed half a dozen of the keys, flipped an entire rank of switches. A siren sounded; the lights brightened and dimmed. From wall apertures, a pale-pink gas began hissing into the room. The receptionist screeched.

"Don't worry, I'm not violent," Lafayette yelled. "All I want is out? Which way?"

"Don't come near me, you maniac!"

Lafayette dashed to the section of wall through which he had entered, began feeling over it frantically as alarm horns hooted behind him. Abruptly, a panel rotated open on a dimly glowing chamber. Lafayette stepped through; the panel slammed behind him. A green light glowed on the opposite wall. There was a momentary sensation as if his brain had come loose from its moorings and was whirling at high speed inside his skull. Then darkness exploded around him.

He drifted among luminous flotsam and jetsam,
straining every sense . . .

*. . . tinky-tinky-tinky . . .*

*. . . you think you're the only bird in town with a pair o'
them—*

*. . . where are you? Come in, dear boy, if you hear me.
Come in, come in . . .*

A vast, softly glowing construction of puce and magenta
noodles swept grandly past, rotating slowly; a swarm of
luminous blue-green BB shot veered close, passed him by;
something vast and insubstantial as glowing smoke
swelled before him, swirled around him with a crackle of
static, was gone. A jittering assemblage of red-hot wires
came tumbling from dark distances, swerved to intercept
him. He back-pedaled, making frantic swimming motions,
but it closed on him, was all about him, clinging, penetrat-
ing.

It was as though a hundred and seventy pounds of warm
wax were being injected into his skin, painlessly squeezing
him out through the pores.

*"Aha! Got you, you bodynapper!"* a silent voice yelled in
both ears at once.

"Hey—wait!" O'Leary shouted. "Can't we discuss
this?"

*Wait, nothing! Out! Out!*

For a moment O'Leary saw a vengeful face—the same
face he had seen in the glass in Belarius' office—glaring at
him. Then he was sliding away into emptiness.

"Wait! Help! I have to get word to Nicodaeus!"

*"Leave me drifting in Limbo, you will . . ."* the voice
came back faintly.

"Raunchini! Don't leave me here! I've got to get
back . . ."

"*How* . . ." the voice came faintly, receding, "*do you know my name*—*" The voice was gone. Lafayette shouted—or not shouted, he realized; *transmitted*, in some way he would figure out later, after he was safe back home. But there was no answer; only faint, ghostly voices all around:

. . . *told him no, but you know how men are* . . .

. . . *oopy-toopy-foopy-foom* . . .

*Nine . . . eight . . . seven* . . .

*DEAR BOY! IS IT REALLY YOU? I'D ABOUT GIVEN UP HOPE!*

"Help!" Lafayette yelled. He was rotating end over end now—or was it the other way around? He could feel his sense of identity draining away like oil from a broken pot; his thoughts were growing weaker, vaguer, the voices fainter . . . *HOLD ON, LAD . . . JUST A FEW SECONDS LONGER . . . DON'T GIVE UP THE SHIP* . . .

Something as intangible as smoke brushed over him; a vague fog-shaped loomed, enveloped him like a shadowy fist. A sense of pressure, a burst of light—then darkness. . . .

3

He was lying on a hard, lumpy surface, itching furiously. He made a move to scratch, and discovered that both knees were bandaged, as well as both elbows and his chin.

He struggled to a sitting position. In the faint moonlight that filtered down through the leaves overhead, he saw that he was neatly enclosed in a cage made of lashed poles. He had been lying, he saw, on an ancient mattress with a stained striped ticking; there was a bowl of water beside him, and what appeared to be gnawed crusts of bread. He sniffed; the odors hanging in the air—of unwashed laundry, goat cheese, and woodsmoke—were somehow

107

familiar. His legs and arms ached, his back ached, his neck ached.

"I must be black-and-blue all over," he grunted. "Where am I? What's happened to me?"

There was a soft sound of footsteps; a familiar figure approached.

"Gizelle!" O'Leary's voice broke with relief. "Am I glad to see you! Get me out of here!"

The girl stood with hands on hips, looking down at him with a unreadable expression. "Zorro?" she said doubtfully.

O'Leary groaned. "I know, I look like a fellow named Raunchini. But it's really me—not really Zorro, but the fellow you thought was Zorro—only I was actually Lafayette O'Leary, of course. But I'll explain all that later."

"You don't theenk you're a beeg bird anymore? You don't try to jump off cleefs, flapping your arms?"

"What? I didn't jump off the cliff, I fell—and—"

Gizelle smiled; she turned, whistled shrilly. Voices responded. A moment later Luppo's hulking figure appeared. He stared at O'Leary with an expression like a Doberman awaiting the kill order.

"Why deed you wheestle?" he grunted. "Ees he—"

"He said he ees heemself—Zorro!"

"Of course I'm myself—in a manner of speaking," Lafayette snapped. "But—oh, well, never mind. You wouldn't understand. Just let me out of here, pronto!"

"Uh-huh—that's heem," Luppo said.

"Good! Een that case—when the sun rises—we can proceed!" Gizelle cried ecstatically.

"Oh, look here, Gizelle—you're not going to start that wedding business all over again?" Lafayette protested.

Luppo looked at him, a gold tooth shining in his crooked grin. "Not quite," he said. "Would you believe . . . . the Death of the Thousand Hooks?"

"Eet weel be very exciting, Zorito," Gizelle informed Lafayette, leaning close to his cage to hiss the words in his face. "First weel be the feexing of the hooks. Een the old days, there was just one beeg hook, you know—but naturally we've been making progress. Now we use leetle beety feesh hooks—hundreds and hundreds of theem. We steeck theem een—slowly—all over you. Then we tie a streeng to each one, and leeft you up eento the air weeth theem—"

"Gizelle—spare me the details!" O'Leary groaned. "If I'm Zorro, I already know all this—and if I'm not, I'm innocent, and you ought to free me. You ought to free me anyway; what's a nice girl like you doing mixed up in a dirty business like this, anyway?"

"Free you? A feelthy peeg who takes advantage of a poor girl who ees fool enough to love heem?"

"I've told you—I'm not myself! I mean I'm not really Zorro! I mean—I *am* Zorro—physically—but actually I'm Lafayette O'Leary! I'm just occupying Zorro's body for the moment! Under the circumstances it wouldn't be ethical for me to marry you. Can't you see that?"

"First you made me streep; theen you sneaked out like a policeman een the night, and locked me een my own boudoir! A meellion feesh hooks could not repay me for the pangs I have suffered for you, you . . . sheep een wolf's clothing!"

"Why didn't you do the job while I was out of my mind? Then I wouldn't have known anything about it."

"What? Mistreat a holy man, affleected of Dumballa? You theenk we are barbarians?"

"Yeah—it would have been pretty tough on Tazlo Haz. The poor boob wouldn't have had a clue what was going on."

"Tazlo Haz—that's what you kept screeching wheen

you were trying to fly," Gizelle said. "What does eet mean?"

"It's my name. I mean it was Zorro's name—or the name of the ego that shifted into Zorro's body when I shifted into his. He's a birdman—with wings, you know." Lafayette fingered his skinned knees gingerly. "I guess it was as hard for him to realize his wings were gone as it was for me to walk through walls."

"Zorito—you are a beeg liar—for theese I geeve you credit," Gizelle said. "But eet's not enough. Now I'm going to get a leettle beauty sleep; I want to look my best for you tomorrow—while you're hanging from the hooks." She turned and hurried away; O'Leary wasn't sure whether there had been a break in her voice on the last words or not.

5

Lafayette slumped in the corner of the cage, his aching head resting on his bandaged knees.

"I must be getting old," he thought drearily. "I used to be able to land on my feet—but now I just stumble from one disaster to the next. If I could just explain to somebody, just once, what's actually going on—but somehow, nobody will listen. Everybody seems to hear what they want to hear—or what they expect to hear."

He shifted position. The moon was low in the sky now. It would be daylight in another couple of hours. He might last for a few more hours after that, but by lunchtime it would be all over—if he was lucky. The trestle tables set up under the trees would be laden with roast turkey and hams and nine-layer chocolate cakes, and pitchers of foaming ale; the holiday crowd would feast merrily, with his dangling body as the principal object of merriment. And back in Artesia City, Daphne would be snuggling up with . . .

"Oh, no, she's not," he reminded himself. "That's one consolation anyway. She's in Central, being trained as a rookie agent."

*Yeah—but why?*

"Well—maybe she got worried and dialed Central, reported that I was missing—"

*Uh—uh. There was nothing in the record about that. Belarius checked.*

"Maybe—" Lafayette felt cold fingers clutch at his chest. "Maybe that wasn't really Daphne! Maybe somebody's stolen *her* body, too!"

*Guesswork! That won't get you anywhere. Stick to the point!*

"Great! What *is* the point?"

*The point is you've got about two hours to live unless you do something fast!*

"But what?" he groaned between gritted teeth. "So far I've been a leaf in the storm, tossed this way and that by events that have been running wild, out of control. I've got to take over and start running things *my* way for a change. And the first item is to get out of here . . ."

He prowled the cage for the fiftieth time, inspecting every joint—and found them all as securely lashed with rawhide as the last time. He checked each stout rail; the smallest was as big as his arm at the elbow, with room between them barely sufficient to pass a water cup. He tried again to rock the cage, on the chance that tipping it would open a seam; it was like rocking a bank vault.

"All right, without a knife direct measures are out. What about more sophisticated techniques? Like focusing the Physical Energies, for example . . ."

O'Leary closed his eyes, marshaled his thoughts.

*It's worked before. It's how you got to Artesia in the first place, remember? And how you met Daphne. Remember how you wished for a bathtub, and got one—complete with occupant? She certainly looked charming, wearing nothing but soapsuds and a pretty smile. And later, in the pink and silver gown, facing the*

111

*duchess . . . and later yet, snuggling up in the dark . . .*

"But this isn't getting me out of this cage," he reminded himself sternly. "Think about the time you produced a Coke machine when you were dying of thirst in the desert, on your way to Lod's stronghold. Or about conjuring up Dinny, when I needed a ride. I got a dinosaur instead of a horse, true, but as it turned out, that was a lucky break . . ."

*Stop reminiscing!* he commanded himself. *You were going to focus your Physhical Energies, remember?*

"I can't," he muttered. "Central put an end to all that with their blasted Suppressor. Let's face it, I'm stuck."

*That's what you thought when you were in Melange, too—but you were wrong!*

"Sure—but that was a special case. I was in another Locus, the rules were changed . . ."

*Try! This is no time to give up!*

"Well . . ." Lafayette closed his eyes, pictured a sharp-bladed pocket knife lying in the corner of the cage. *Under some litter,* he specified, *in a spot where I wouldn't have seen it. I haven't acutally scraped around over there; I don't KNOW there isn't a knife . . . So BE there, knife! A nice little barlow with a bone handle. . . .*

If there was a small quiver in the even flow of entropy, he failed to detect it.

"But that doesn't mean it didn't work," he said bravely. "Take a look . . ." He went to the corner in question, scraped away the drifted leaves and bird droppings and straw, exposing bare planks.

"No knife," he mumbled. "It figures. My luck's run out. I didn't have a chance from the beginning. I can see that now."

*Sure. But why? Maybe if you could figure out why, you'd have a chance of fighting back.*

"Why? How do I know? Because somebody wanted me out of the way, I suppose."

*Why not just knock you in the head, in that case? Why all this business of turning you into Zorro?*

112

"Maybe . . . maybe that was just a side effect. If it wasn't just you that was turned into Zorro; if Zorro was also turned into *you*—and it seems like a logical assumption—if you can call any part of this insanity logical . . ."

*Then—the whole idea might have been to get Zorro into my body—and I was just dumped into his to get me out of the way.*

"It's a possibility."

*But why? What would that accomplish?*

"For one thing—assuming Zorro's the culprit—it would put him in the palace right now, occupying your place, using your clothes, your toothbrush, your bed—"

*Let's drop that line of thought for the moment! OK, so Zorro found a way to steal bodies. He conned the Red Bull into handing me the Mark III Shape Changer, and I was boob enough to push the button. Then what? It still doesn't explain things like the Stasis Pod, and the old geezer in blue robes. . . .*

"Ye Gods!" O'Leary blurted. "That's who the photo was, back in Belarius' office! The old man in the tank—but without the beard!"

6

*Now we're getting somewhere,* Lafayette assured himself. *We've established a connection between Central and Artesia, that Central—or at least Belarius—doesn't seem to know anything about.*

"Right—and if you recall, he got a bit paranoid as soon as he caught you staring at the photo of . . . what did he call him? Jorlemagne. Wanted you to rat on him, spill the beans—implying you were in it with him—whatever 'it' is."

*But that doesn't explain why this Jorlemagne was lying around in a cave like Sleeping Beauty in an electronic*

113

*bunk bed making strange noises at anybody who disturbs him.*

"Wait a minute; let's see what we've got: Back at Central, there's been some skulduggery. Belarius is upset about something done by Jorlemagne, who's dropped out of sight. This may or may not tie in with the Focal Referent, which Belarius may not know anything about, probably the latter, since he's under the impression it weighs umpteen tons . . ."

*Wait a minute. It seems I remember him correcting me when I called it a Mark III. He insisted it was a Mark II. So . . .*

"So—maybe what you had was a new model, miniaturized. But—why wouldn't Belarius know that? After all, he's Chief of Research, and the Focal Referent was his baby."

*I don't know. But at the same time he's having trouble with this Jorlemagne absconding—presumably with a new model FR than even Belarius knows about—funny things started happening in Artesia. And Artesia in where Jorlemagne is. So—*

"So all I have to do is get to a phone and dial my special number, and tell them where to pick up their boy!"

*Fine—except you'll still be Zorro—and somebody else with your face will be filling in for you at home!*

"Maybe Central can fix that, too."

"I can't wait that long! I have to get back and see what's going on! There's got to be a reason for that sneaking phony to have stolen my body! I want to know what it is!"

*Meanwhile—how do you get out of this cage?*

"Yeah—there *is* that," O'Leary muttered. "I can't cut my way out—and I can't wish myself out. It looks like the end of the trail. Damn! And just when I was beginning to see a little light."

*There's still a lot of loose ends. What about Lom—the kindly old gent who picked you up and fed you—and then picked your pocket?*

114

"Yeah—what about him? Bavarian ham, yet. And Danish butter. Nobody in Artesia ever heard of Denmark or Bavaria. Or New Orleans, either!" O'Leary smacked his fist into his palm. "It's obvious! Lom's a Central agent, too."

*And when he found the Focal Referent on you—he naturally assumed you were the thief—or that you were in it with Jorlemagne—*

"So he took steps to get rid of you. Dumped you in Thallathlone."

*Uh-huh. But I got away—by a fluke—and wound up back here. Nice work, O'Leary. Which is better—a nice cool cell in Thallathlone, or the Death of the Thousand Hooks?*

"In another few hours it won't matter, one way or another," O'Leary sighed. "Well, I've had a nice run, while it lasted, but it had to end. I parlayed it from a dull job in a foundry to six years of high living in a palace; I guess I should be satisfied with that. Even if I'd know how it would end, I wouldn't want to change it. Except maybe this last part. It seems like a dirty way to go. This is one time the miracle isn't going to happen. But since there's no hope the least I can do is pull myself together and die like a man."

The moon had set; through the inky black, Lafayette could see nothing except the glow of the guard fire a hundred yards away, and a single candle in a wagon window.

Something passed between Lafayette and the light. Stealthy footsteps sounded from the darkness, coming toward him.

"Hey," he protested, discovering a sudden obstruction in his throat. "It's not time yet."

"Hssst!" Someone was at the bars—a small, silvery-haired figure.

"Lom!"

"Quite right, my boy. Sorry I took so long." There was a rasp of steel against hard leather; a knifeblade threw

115

back a glint from the distant fire. Lashings parted; bars were pulled aside. Lafayette crawled through, ignoring the pain in his scraped knees.

"Let's be off," Lom whispered. "You and I have things to discuss, my lad."

# CHAPTER EIGHT

## 1

The stars were fading in the first gray paling of the dawn. Lafayette huddled, shivering, beside the tiny fire Lom had built under a sheltering rock ledge.

"Sorry there's no coffee this time," the old gentleman said. "You look as though you need it, indeed."

"New Orleans style?" O'Leary queried.

"Umm. Rather good, wasn't it? Never fear, we'll soon be back at my digs, and—"

"They don't have New Orleans coffee in Artesia, Lom—or German ham, either."

"I'm afraid I don't quite understand . . ." Lom looked genuinely puzzled.

"New Orleans is in Locus Alpha Nine-three. So is Bavaria—and Denmark."

Lom shook his head. "Dear lad, I merely read what it said on the labels. I don't even know what an old Orleans is, to say nothing of a New one."

"Where did you get the stuff, Lom? There's no handy supermarket around the corner from that peak of yours."

There was a pause.

"Oh, dear." Lom said.

"Well?"

"I . . . I should have known it was wrong. But after all—there seemed to be no owner. There it was, piled in

117

the cave—and—and I—well, I appropriated it. My only defense is . . . I was hungry."

"You *found* it?"

"Please believe me. It would be dreadful if you got the wrong impression."

"Yes—wouldn't it . . ."

"Are you hinting at something?"

"Not hinting, Lom. I want to know where you fit into all this."

"You're being frightfully obscure, my boy—"

"I'm not your boy—in spite of your rescuing me. Come clean, Lom: what do you want from me?"

"I? Why, nothing at all. I felt responsible for you, in a way, and did my best to help you—"

"How did you find me?" Lafayette cut in.

"Ah—as to that, I employed a simple device called a Homer. It makes bipping sounds, you see, and—"

"More electronic gadgets, eh? Where'd you get it?"

"Concealed in a small grotto."

"Grotto?"

"Cave. I hope I didn't do wrong by using it to save you from a horrible death—"

"Another lucky find, eh? That's your answer to everything. Well, I suppose it's possible. Every cave in Artesia seems to be stuffed full of loot. But that still doesn't explain how you carried me from wherever I landed up to that eagle's nest. A mountain goat couldn't have climbed those cliffs, even without me on his back."

"Climb— Oh, I see what you were thinking! No, no, I should have explained. You see—there's a stairway. An escalator, as a matter of fact. No trick at all, just had to drag you a few feet and push the button." Lom beamed.

"Oh, that clears everything up," Lafayette said. "Swell. You didn't climb, you used the escalator. How stupid of me not to have figured that one out."

"You—you sound dubious."

"Who are you, Lom!" O'Leary demanded. "Where do you come from? Why did you cut me out of that cage?"

Lom drew a breath, hesitated, let it out in a sigh. "I," he

118

said in a dismal tone, "am a failure." He looked across the flickering fire at Lafayette. "Once, I occupied a . . . a position of considerable trust. Then . . . things went badly for me. There was a robbery, so arranged as to make it appear that I—that I was the thief. I escaped barely ahead of the authorities."

"And?"

"I . . . made my way here. Foraging, I stumbled on the, er, supplies of which you know; I found the route to my isolated hideaway. Then—*you* dropped from the skies. I naturally did what I could for you."

"Then?"

"Then you disappeared. Poof! I searched for you—and at last I found you, as you know. And here we are."

"You left out one small item. What did you do with the Mark III?"

"Mark who?"

"Maybe you didn't make off with the till, back where you came from," O'Leary said. "But there was a gadget concealed in a secret pocket of my coat. You took it while I was unconscious. I want it back."

Lom was shaking his head emphatically. "You wrong me, my boy—"

"Just call me O'Leary."

"Is that your name?" Lom asked quickly.

"Certainly—"

"Then why did you tell the young women—the one who seemed to dislike you so—that it was Zorro?"

"Because it is. I mean, she knows me as Zorro—"

"But that's not your real name? Curious that you have the letter Z embroidered on your shirt pocket—and on your handkerchief—and your socks."

"I'm in disguise," Lafayette said. "Don't try to change the subject. Where's the Mark III?"

"Tell me about it," Lom suggested.

"I'll tell you this much," Lafayette snapped. "It's the most dangerous object in the country! I don't know why you wanted it; maybe you thought you could pawn it; but—"

"Mr. O'Leary—I took nothing from your person, while you were asleep or any other time!"

"Don't stall, Lom! I want it back!"

"You may search me if you wish; you're considerably larger and stronger than I. I can't stop you."

"What good would that do? You could have hidden it."

"Indeed! And why, if I had robbed you, would I have returned to preserve you from what, it appeared, would have been a peculiarly unpleasant fate?"

"Maybe you needed me to show you how to operate it."

"I see. Without letting on I had it, I suppose."

"Well, blast it," O'Leary snarled, "if I didn't take it, where is it?"

"Possibly," Lom said thoughtfully, "it dropped from your pocket when you fell. . . ."

There was a momentary silence, while Lafayette stared across the fire at the small, indignant figure, who returned the look defiantly.

"All right," O'Leary sighed. "I can't prove you took it. I guess I ought to apologize. And to thank you for getting me out of that cage."

"Perhaps," Lom said, "if you told me a bit more about the missing item?"

"Forget it, Lom. The less anybody knows about it, the better."

"This Mark III; was it your property? Or were you keeping it for someone else?"

"Don't pry, Lom! Tell me: in your explorations, did you come across a cave with, ah, with anything, oh, like a sort of box in it?"

"Since you won't answer my questions, O'Leary, why should I answer yours?"

"Because I need to get to the bottom of this, that's why! There's a plot afoot, Lom! Bigger than anything you could imagine! And I'm mixed up in it! And I want out!"

"Oh? In that case, why not tell me all you know—"

"Never mind." O'Leary got painfully to his feet. "I've got to get going, Lom. Time's a-wasting. I have to make contact with—" He broke off. "With some friends of mine," he finished.

"Suppose I go with you," Lom suggested, jumping up.

"Out of the question," Lafayette said. "I don't mean to be rude, but I can't afford to be slowed down. Beside which it might be dangerous."

"I don't mind. And I'll do my best to keep to the pace."

"Look, Lom, you're far better off right here. You have your hut, and you can live on leaves and berries and Bavarian ham, in peace and quiet—"

"I still have hopes," Lom cut in, "of clearing my name. Possibly these friends you mentioned could help me."

"King Shosto and his boys will be combing the woods for me. If they catch you in my company they'll probably allocate five hundred of those hooks to you."

"I doubt it, lad. I know the trails through these hills quite well. In fact, without me to guide you, I doubt if you'll ever reach the city."

"Well—come on then. I can't stop you. But don't expect me to wait for you." He turned away.

"Wait!" Lom said sharply. "Not that way, Mr. O'Leary." He stepped forward and parted the bushes to reveal a narrow path leading down the rocky slope. "Shall we go?"

2

Twice in the hour before sunrise, O'Leary and Lom were forced to take refuge in deep shrubbery while a party of Wayfarers thrashed their way through the underbrush close at hand. From their conversation it was apparent that there would be plenty of hooks to go around when the owner of the footprints near the broached cage was apprehended along with the escaped prisoner.

"Tsk. Such an uncharitable attitude," Lom commented

121

as they emerged from their last concealment.

"Just wait until I get my hands on this Zorro character," Lafayette said. "He's the one at the bottom of this—"

"I thought *you* were Zorro?" Lom said sharply.

"Not really. I just look like him. I mean—well, never mind. It's too complicated."

He turned to see Lom staring hard at his thumb, which he was solemnly waggling.

"Playing with your fingers?" O'Leary snapped.

"Ah—not at all, my boy," Lom said, thrusting both hands into his pockets. "Tell me—what will you do when we reach the city?"

"I'll have to play it be ear. Once inside the palace, if I can just get a word with Adoranne . . ."

"Frankly, my boy—you look a trifle disreputable. Your garments are somewhat the worse for wear, and it appears you haven't shaved of late, and that gold earring in your left ear is hardly calculated to inspire confidence."

"I'll think of something. I'll have to."

As the sun cleared the treetops, they emerged from the woods onto a stretch of sloping pastureland dotted with peaceful cows, which gazed placidly at them as they tramped down to the road. A passing steam-powered wain gave them a lift to the city limits. As they walked through the cobbled street, redolent of early-morning odors of roasting coffee and fresh-baked bread, a few early risers gave them curious looks. They paused at a sidewalk stall within sight of the palace towers, rosy-tinted in the early light, for a quick breakfast of eggs, bacon, toast and jam, which seemed to Lafayette to drop into an empty cavern the size of a municipal car-barn.

"It's amazing what a little food will do," he commented, as he finished off his second cup of coffee. "Suddenly, everything seems simpler. I'll go to the palace gates, explain that I have important information, and request an audience. Then, after I've told Adoranne a few things that could only be known to me—I'll explain who I am. After that it will be routine. By this time tomorrow, everything will be straightened out."

"I take it you know this Princess Adoranne personally?"

"Certainly. We're old friends. In fact, I was engaged to her once; but I realized in the nick of time that it was really Daphne I was in love with—"

"You—engaged to a princess?" Lom was looking highly skeptical.

"Sure—why not?"

Lom's mouth tightened. "Mr. O'Leary—this is hardly the time for leg-pulling. After all, if we've joined forces—"

"Who says we've joined forces? I let you come along for the ride, that's all, Lom. I still have no reason to trust you. In fact, I think this is where our paths should part. You go your way and I'll go mine."

"You promised to introduce me to your, ah, influential friends," Lom said quickly.

"Oh, no, I didn't." Lafayette shook his head. "That was *your* idea."

"See here, O'Leary—or Zorro—or whatever your name might be," Lom said testily. "I can be of help to you; suppose you have difficulty in gaining entrance to the palace—"

"Don't worry about that; I'll manage."

"Then you intend to—to repay my efforts on your behalf by abandoning me here?"

"Why put it like that? I'll tell you what, Lom; if everything goes well, I'll look you up afterward, and see what I can do for you, all right?"

"I want to do something—something positive, to demonstrate my usefulness. Now, if I go with you to the palace—"

"Out of the question. I might be able to talk myself inside, but you . . . well, candidly, Lom, you don't look particularly impressive, you know, in those tattered clothes and needing a haircut."

"Surely there's *something* I can do?"

123

"Well—all right, if you insist. Go find the Red Bull. Bring him to the palace. No, on second thought, make it the Ax and Dragon. If I flunk out at the palace, I'll meet you there. And if I make it—I'll send for you. OK?"

"Well . . . I'll do my best. The Red Bull, you say?"

"Sure. Ask around. Any pickpocket in town can help you. Now I've got to be off." Lafayette rose, paid for their breakfast with the lone silver dollar he had found in Zorro's pocket, and set off at a purposeful stride toward the palace.

3

The brass-helmeted guard, resplendent in baggy blue knee pants and a yellow-and-blue-striped coat gave O'Leary a lazy up-and-down look.

"Get hence, Jack, before I run you in for loitering," he suggested curtly.

"I'm here on business," Lafayette said. "I have important news for Princess Adoranne."

"Oh, yeah?" The man shifted his harquebus casually. "What about?"

"Classified," O'Leary said. "Look here, we're wasting time. Just pass my request along to the sergeant of the guard."

"Oh, a wise one, eh?" The sentry growled. "Beat it, Greaser, while you still got the chanst."

"Like that, huh?" Lafayette said. He cupped his hands to his mouth:

"Sergeant of the Guard, post number one—on the double!"

"Why, you—"

"Ah-ah—don't do anything rash," O'Leary cautioned as the enraged man raised his bell-mouthed gun. "Witnesses, remember?"

"All right, what's this all about?" a short, plump noncom with a handlebar mustache swaggered into view. He halted, looked Lafayette up and down. His face turned an alarming shade of purple.

"Shorty!" Lafayette cried. "Am I glad to see you!"

"Grab that bum!" the sergeant roared. "That's the lousy punk that clobbered three o' my boys here Monday a week!"

4

It was difficult, Lafayette conceded, to keep his voice cool, calm, and reasonable with three large men clamping his arms in pretzel-like positions behind his back, while dragging him across the cobbled courtyard. Still, it was no time to give way to intemperate language.

"If you'd just—*ow!*—listen to what I have to say—*ouch!*—I'm sure you'll agree that what I have to report—*unh!*—is worth listening to."

"Yeah? Give him another quarter turn, LaVerne!"

"Shorty—at least give me a hearing—"

"That's Sergeant to you, crum-bum!" the five-foot-three harquebusier bellowed. "You can tell it to the judge—next month, when he gets back from his vacation!"

"I can't wait a month! It's an emergency!"

"If he says anything else, LaVerne—stick a bandanna in his mouth. The one you use to mop off the back o' your neck on hot afternoons!"

They passed the stables, the harness room, turned into the serviceway that ran beside the royal pigpen. The guards recoiled as the imprisoned boar emitted a loud snort and threw his quarter-ton bulk against the fence.

"What's got into George?" LaVerne inquired. "He ain't been hisself for a couple of weeks now."

"Maybe he knows we got a barbecue planned for next month, someone suggested.

"Nothing ain't been normal lately," LaVerne mourned. "Not since—"

"Belay that!" Shorty yelled. "You slobs are at attention!"

Lafayette's escort hustled him up three steps into a small squad-room lit even at this hour by a forty-watt bulb dangling from a kinked cord. An unshaven man in shirt sleeves sat with a boot propped on a battered desk, picking his teeth with a short dagger. He raised a sardonic eyebrow and reached for a form.

"Book this mug on suspicion, Sarge," Shorty said.

"Ssupicion o' what?"

"Suit yourself. Forgery, maybe. Or Peeping Tom. Or watering wine. Just hold him while I work up a file on him that'll keep him on ice until they pension me off."

"This has gone far enough," Lafayette spoke up. "While you flatfoots jabber, the kingdom may be lost. I have to see Princess Adoranne, right now!"

The desk sergeant listened with his mouth slightly open. He looked Lafayette up and down, then turned an unfriendly eye on the mustachioed noncom who had arrested him.

"What's the idea bringing a loony in here?" he demanded. "You know all them nut cases go direct to the filbert factory—"

"Call Princess Adoranne," Lafayette said in a voice which cracked slightly in spite of his efforts. "Just request Her Highness to come down for a moment, all right?" He tried a friendly smile, which caused the desk sergeant to edge backward.

"Hold him, boys," he muttered. "He's getting ready to go violent." He dinged a bell on the desk; a door opened and an uncombed head of shaggy pale hair appeared, surmounting the thick-lipped, puffy-eyed face of a deputy.

"Oglethorp, slap a set of irons on this pigeon," he said. "Throw him in dungeon number twelve, at the back. We don't want him yelling and getting everybody upset—"

"Irons?" Lafayette yelled. "I'll have the lot of you pounding beats on the graveyard shift!" He jerked free, eluded a grab, made a dive for the door, hooked a foot over an outthrust ankle and witnessed the finest display of pyrotechnics since the previous Third of October —Artesian Independence Day.

Hard hands were clamped on his arms, hauling him upward. He tried to move his legs, then let them drag. He was aware of descending stairs, of tottering along a dark, evil-smelling corridor, of a heavy iron gate being lifted. A shove sent him stumbling into a low-ceilinged room that stank of burning kerosene from the flambeaux mounted in brackets along the wall.

"I'm S'Laf'yet 'Leary," he mumbled, shaking his head to clear it. "I demand a lawyer. I demand to see Adoranne. I demand to send a message to my wife, Countess Daphne—" He broke off as his arms were twisted up behind him and held in a double come-along grip.

"Looks like the booze has rotted his wits out," the blond turnkey said, exhaling a whiskey breath into O'Leary's ear.

"Stick him in number twelve, Percy. All the way in the back."

"Sure, Oglethorpe—but, geeze, I ain't swept twelve out in a while, an'—"

"Never mind coddling the slob. He's one o' them Peeping Irvings."

"Yeah? Geeze, Oglethorpe, is he the one they spotted last month, climbing the ivy fer a glimpse o' Princess Adoranne taking a shower?"

"Never mind that, Percy! Lock him up, and get back to yer comic book!"

Percy, Lafayette noted vaguely, was even larger and less intellectual looking than Oglethorpe. He allowed himself to be prodded along to the end of the dark passage, stood leaning dizzily against the wall as the jailer selected an oversized key from the ring at his belt.

"Say, pal . . . uh . . . how was it?" the lout inquired in confidential tones as he removed the handcuffs. "I mean . . . does her Highness look as neat in the nood as a guy would figger?"

"Neater," Lafayette said blurrily, rubbing his head.

127

"That is . . . it's none of your business. But listen—this is all an error, you understand? A case of mistaken identity. I have to get a message to Countess Daphne or the Princess, and—"

"Yeah." The jailer nodded. As he thrust Lafayette into the tiny cell, from which a goaty odor wafted, O'Leary hardly noticed his hand brushing the other's side, his fingers nimbly plucking something away, palming it. . . .

"That's why you was climbing the ivy, sure," Percy rambled on sardonically. "It's as good of a alibi as any, punk. I bet you never even glommed nothing."

"That's what you think!" Lafayette yelled, as the door slammed. He pressed his face against the bars set in the foot-square opening in the metal slab. "I'll make a deal: you deliver my message, and I'll tell you all about it!"

"Yeah?" Percy replied, somewhat doubtfully. "How do I know you ain't lying?"

"Even if I make it up, it'll be better than a comic book," Lafayette snapped.

"Nuts," Percy said loftily. "And anyway—the whole conversation is in lousy taste, considering."

"Considering what?"

"Considering the shape her Highness is in." The jailer's lower lip thrust out. "Ain't it a crying shame?"

"Ain't what—I mean isn't what a crying shame?"

"That the Princess is laying at death's door—down wit' a fever which nobody don't know how to cure it—that's what! And Count Alain and the Lady Daphne along wit' her!"

"Did you say—at death's door?" O'Leary choked.

"Right, Bub. They say all took sick at once—a fortnight since—and they ain't expected to recover. That's how come King Lafayette had to take over."

"K-King Lafayette?"

"Sure. And the first thing he done was to beef up the guard force, which I was one o' the first hired. Where you been, anyways?"

"But . . . but . . . but . . ."

"Yeah—so don't crack wise," Percy said with dignity. "So long, hotshot. See you in Death Row."

Lafayette sat on the heap of damp straw that was the cell's only furnishings, numbly fingering the knobs on his skull.

"Things couldn't go this wrong," he mumbled. "I must be the one who's feverish. I'm delirious, imagining all this. Actually, I'm in bed, being tended by Daphne—"

He broke off. "Hey," he said thoughtfully. "Daphne can't be sick in bed—I saw her at Central, going through rookie training, yesterday!" He jumped up, banged on the bars until Percy appeared with a napkin tucked in his collar, wiping his chin.

"You said that Countess Daphne's been sick in bed for two weeks?"

"Yeah, that's right."

"And she hasn't recovered?"

"Nope. Nor likely to, poor kid."

"How do you know? Did you see her?"

"Now I know you're loopy, Rube. I'll get a squint at her Ladyship in bed right after I get my promotion to Buck Admiral."

"Who says she's sick?"

Percy spread his thick hands. "It's what they call common knowledge. King Lafayette kept it quiet for a couple days, but then he had to let the word out, on account of everybody was getting a little uptight on account of they didn't see the Princess around and about, like." Percy took out a bone toothpick and gouged at a back tooth.

"Have you seen this King Lafayette?" O'Leary asked.

"Sure; I seen him yesterday, reviewing the guard. The poor guy looked pretty bad off, and I guess it figgers, wit' that snazzy little piece Countess Daphne about to croak, an' all—"

"What did he look like?"

"You know—kind of a skinny, long-legged kid wit' a

bunch o' curly brown hair and a sort o' snappy smile—only he wasn't smiling yesterday. Boy, what a temper!" Percy shook his head admiringly. "The boys tell me it's the first time he ever had anybody horsewhipped, too."

"He's horsewhipping people?"

"Sure. Well, the poor slob's got a lot on his mind, like. I guess that's why he kicked the cat—"

"He kicked a cat?"

"Uh-huh. Tried to, anyways. I always heard he was a good-natured bozo, but I guess having your frail croak on you is enough to kind of give anybody a little edge on. That, and the war." Percy inspected his toothpick gravely.

"What war?"

"Geeze, Bub, you're really out of it, ain't you? The war wit' the Vandals, natcherly."

"You mean—Artesia's at war?"

"Naw—not yet. But any day now. See, these Vandals, they got this invasion planned, which they want to take over the country so's they can loot and rob and all. What they'll do, they'll kill off all the men, and capture all the broads—"

"Who says so?"

"Huh? King Lafayette said so—the first day after he had hisself coronated on account of the Princess being laid up—"

"When is all this supposed to happen?"

"Any day now. That's why everybody's got to turn in their cash and jewels, for the like war effort. Boy, you should of seen some o' the rich merchants howl when us boys was sent out to make some collections." Percy wagged his head. "Some o' them bums got no patriotism."

Lafayette groaned.

"Yeah, it's a heartbreaker, ain't it, pal?" Percy belched comfortably. "Well, it's about time fer my relief, Rube. Hang loose—as the executioner said to the customer just before he sprang the trap." Percy sauntered off, whistling. Lafayette tottered to a corner and sank down. Things were beginning to come into focus now. The plot was bigger and better organized than anything he'd imagined. There

130

was an invasion, all right—but not from outside. The invader had saved a lot of time and effort by going right to the heart of things; it was a neat switch: invade the palace first, and take over the country at leisure.

"But how did he do it?" Lafayette got to his feet and paced.

"Let's say this Zorro stumbled onto some loot stashed by Goruble; Lom said the hills are full of caves full of the stuff. So—he got his hands on the Mark III, discovered what it would do. He got to the Red Bull, and planted the infernal thing on me, knowing I'd be boob enough to push the button. When I did, he hurried off to the palace and took up where I left off. Only—" He paused at a thought.

"Only he didn't fool Daphne. Good girl! She smelled a rat, went to the secret phone in Nicodaeus' old lab, and called Central. They picked her up, and she reported . . . reported . . ." Lafayette paused, scratching his chin.

"What could she report? She noticed something wrong; she knows I never kick cats. But she had no way of knowing I was really this Zorro, masquerading as me. She'd just think that somebody had hypnotized me, or something. Whatever she said, she'd have a hard time getting those bureaucrats to listen. Their policy is minimum interference. If they checked, they'd find everything apparently normal. The most they'd do would be to send an agent in to look over the situation . . ." Lafayette halted and smacked a fist into his palm.

"Of course! What an idiot I was not to have spotted it sooner! Lom! He's a Central agent! That's why he knows all those things he shouldn't know! And no wonder he was suspicious of me! I claimed to be Lafayette O'Leary—the man he was sent here to investigate! No wonder he wanted to come into the city with me! He had to keep an eye on me! Only . . . only why did he let me talk him into splitting to go off on a wild-goose chase after the Red Bull—"

*Well, after all, the Red Bull was involved in this, right? Maybe he saw the chance to get filled in on the details of my story, figuring I'd be available whenever he wanted to get back to me. Or maybe—maybe he'd already become convinced of my innocence—or at least that things were more complicated than they looked—and he had to get off by himself to report back to HQ. That's probably it! He's made his report by now; he ought to show up any minute with a Central Enforcer squad to spring me, and get this whole mess straightened out!*

At that moment there was a clump of boots in the passage. O'Leary struggled to his feet, blinking at the glare of a lantern.

"Whatta ya mean, lost it?" said the heavy voice of Oglethorpe. "OK, OK, I'll use mine. . . ."

An iron key clattered in the lock; the door swung wide. Beyond it, beside the hulking guard, Lafayette saw a small, silver-haired figure.

"OK, OK, let's go chum," Oglethorpe rasped.

"Lom! You finally made it!" Lafayette started forward. A large hand against his chest stopped him in his tracks.

"Don't try nothing dumb, Clyde," Oglethorpe advised him in a patient tone, and administered a shove which sent O'Leary staggering back to rebound from the far wall, just in time to collide with Lom as he was pitched through the door. The heavy gate clanged shut.

"Well, we meet again, my boy," the old fellow said apologetically.

# CHAPTER NINE

## 1

"You mean," Lafayette said in a sagging voice, "you're *not* a Central agent? You weren't sent here to investigate Daphne's report? You don't have an Enforcer squad standing by to put the arm on this bogus King O'Leary?"

Lom frowned at O'Leary. "You almost sound," he said, "as if you hoped I *was* a Central agent . . ."

"You don't deny you know about Central, then?" Lafayette leaped into the breach. "I guess that's something. Look here, Lom—just who *are* you? How do you figure in all this?"

"Just the question I was about to ask you," Lom countered. "Frankly—my previous theories seem somewhat untenable in light of the present contretemps."

"What theories?"

"Not so fast, young fellow," Lom said in an entirely new tone. "I didn't say I was satisfied with your *bona fides*; far from it. As a matter of fact, it's obvious to me now that you're either innocent—a hapless victim—or more deeply involved than I'd thought. I sincerely hope you can establish that the former is the case . . ."

"Wait a minute. You sound as if I was expected to make excuses to *you!* If you're not a Central agent, then you must be in this mess up to your ears!"

"How does it happen," Lom demanded in a no-

nonsense voice, "that you seem to be familiar with a device—the Mark III Focal Referent—which is a secret I had supposed to be known only to its inventor, and one other?"

"Easy; the Red Bull handed it to me—"

"A facile explanation, but hardly satisfying."

"I don't know why I'm alibiing in the first place," O'Leary snapped. "You're the one with some explanations to give. And don't try to snow me with that story about just happening to stumble on a cave full of just what you needed. If Central sent you here, well and good. They'd have supplied you, naturally. If not—then you must know a lot more than you're telling."

"Possibly," Lom said crisply. "Now, tell me: why were you roaming the hills in the first place?"

"What were you doing on the mountaintop?" Lafayette came back.

"Why did you come here to Artesia City? Whom were you expecting to meet?"

"How do you know about Central? Nobody in Artesia ever heard of it, but me, and Daphne!"

"What's *your* connection with Central?"

"I asked you first!"

"What's he paying you?"

"What's who paying me?"

"*Him*, that's who!"

"I don't know what you're talking about!"

"I'll double his offer!"

"Talk or I'll twist that skinny neck of yours!"

"Lay a hand on me and I'll visit you with a plague of cramps!"

"Aha! Now you're a warlock!" Lafayette took a step toward the old man—and doubled up at a stab of pain under the ribs. He made a desperate grab, and yelped as his left calf knotted in a Charley horse.

"I warned you," Lom said calmly.

Lafayette made one more try, was rewarded by a stitch in his side. He lurched back against the bars.

"Now talk," Lom snapped. "I want the whole story.

134

What was your role supposed to be? How did you happen to fall out with him? That's why you fled to the hills, eh? But why did you come back?"

"You're babbling," Lafayette gasped, clutching his ribs. "I'm Lafayette O'Leary. Somebody tricked me . . . into this Zorro routine . . . so they could take my place. . . ."

"Anyone who wanted to masquerade as O'Leary would simply have disposed of his person, not set him free to confuse the issue. No, my lad, it won't do. Now talk! The truth, this time! Or I'll give you a spasm of the eyeballs, a sensation you'll not soon forget!"

"You talk as if . . . you really didn't know," Lafayette managed, between pangs resembling, he suspected, those of imminent childbirth. His fingers encountered an object in an inside pocket, felt over it. He had a sudden, vivid recollection of those same fingers—Zorro's trained fingers—darting out deftly as Percy thrust him into the cell, lifting something from Percy's belt. He drew the object out, focused watery eyes on it.

". . .don't know," Lom was still talking. "Even if I were convinced you were a mere dupe—which I'm not—"

"How," Lafayette cut in, "would you like to escape from this cell?"

"I should like that very well indeed," Lom spat. "But don't change the subject! I—"

"Take this whammy off me . . ." O'Leary panted, "and we'll talk about it."

"Not until you've made a clean breast of it!"

"Did you notice what I'm holding in my hand?"

"No. What difference would—" Lom paused. "It . . . it appears to be a large key of some sort. It's not—it's not the key to this door—"

"It better be—or Zorro's fingers have lost their touch." Lafayette thrust the key out between the bars.

"Careful, my boy! Don't drop it! Bring it back inside, carefully!"

"Untie this knot in my duodenum!"

"I . . . I . . . very well!" Lafayette staggered at the sudden relief of the stomach cramp. "That was a neat trick," he said. "How did you do it?"

"With this." Lom showed an artifact resembling a ball-point pen. "A simple invention of mine. It projects a sound beam of the proper frequency to induce muscular contraction. You see, I confide in you. Now . . . the key, dear boy!"

"Deal," Lafayette said. "A truce between us. We join forces until we find out what's going on."

"Why should I trust you?"

"Because if you don't I'll pitch this key out of reach, and we'll both be stuck here. I won't be able to help Adoranne, maybe—but you won't be free to do her any more harm!"

"I assure you, that's the last thing I desire, lad!"

"Deal?" Lafayette persisted.

"Deal, then. But at the first false move—"

"Let's not waste time," Lafayette said, tossing the key to Lom. "We have some plans to make."

## 2

"Geeze, don't you ever sleep?" Percy inquired aggrievedly as he halted before the cell door. "What you want this time? I told you already chow ain't till one pee em—" He broke off, peering between the bars into the gloomy cell. "Hey—it seems to me like there was another mug in here wit' youse. A little geezer—" He broke off with a grunt, doubled over, and went down. Lafayette thrust the door open and stepped over the prostrate turnkey as Lom came forward from the dark corner where he had lain in wait.

"He'll be all right, won't he?"

"Ummm. I just gave him a touch of *angina*," Lom said offhandedly. "He'll be as good as new in half an hour. Now what?"

"There's still Oglethorpe to deal with. Come on."

Stealthily, the escapees moved along the corridor, past empty cells, to the archway beyond which the corner of the warden's desk was visible, supporting a pair of size-fourteen boots with well-worn soles.

"Give him a shot in the ankle," Lafayette murmured. Lom eased forward, focused his sound projector, pressed the stud. There was a muffled exclamation; a large, hairy hand came down to massage the foot. Lom administered a second dose; with a yelp, Oglethorpe swiveled his chair, swinging his feet out of sight as his head and shoulders rotated into view. Lom took careful aim and zapped him again. The big man roared and slapped his own jaw with a report like a pistol shot. As he jumped up, the old gentleman sighted on his lumbar area and gave him yet another blast. Oglethorpe arched backward, lost his balance, and cracked his head on the desk on the way down.

"Got him," Lom stated with satisfaction.

"You're going to have to simplify that procedure before it replaces a sock full of sand," O'Leary told him. "He made more noise than a rumble between rival gangs armed with garbage can lids."

"Still, we seem to have occasioned no alarm. After all, who would expect a jailbreak at this hour of the day?"

"Well, let's not just stand here congratulating ourselves. We've got ground to cover. Let's take in those lockers and see what's available in the way of disguises."

Five minutes of rummaging turned up a pair of shabby cloaks and a worn canvas pouch full of battered tools.

"We're plumbers," O'Leary said. "I'm the master pipefitter, and you're my assistant—"

"Quite the contrary," Lom interrupted. "A silver-haired apprentice would hardly carry conviction."

"All right—let's not fall out over a jurisdictional dispute." Lafayette adjusted the cloak to cover as much as possible of his grimy silk shirt and baggy satin trousers. In a desk drawer he found the keys to the heavy grate that barred the passage. They lifted it, occasioning a dismal groan of rusty metal, eased under, lowered it back in position. Ten feet farther, the passage branched.

"Which way?" Lom wondered aloud. "I confess I have no sense of direction."

"Come on," O'Leary said, leading the way toward a steep flight of stone stairs. At the top, a cross passage led two ways.

"To the left," Lafayette hissed. "We have to pass the squad room, so take it easy."

"How does it happen," Lom whispered, "that you know your way well?"

"I did time down here the first week I was in Artesia. And since then I've been down a few times to visit friends."

"Hmmm. You know, my boy, at times I'm tempted to believe your story . . ."

"Whether you believe it or not, we're in this together. Now let's go before we're arrested for loitering." Lafayette advanced stealthily, risked a peek into the room. Three harquebusiers were seated around a table spooning up beans, their shirts unbuttoned, their floppy hats laid aside, their rapiers dangling from wooden pegs on the wall. One of the trio looked up; his eyes met O'Leary's.

"Yeah," he barked. "Who youse looking for?"

"Roy," Lafayette said promptly. "He said it was a hurry-up call."

"Shorty ain't on until six pee em. A hurry up call, hey? You must be the vet."

"Right," Lafayette improvised as the man rose and sauntered toward him, hitching at his purple-and-green suspenders. The cop eyed O'Leary's tool bag, prodded it with a thick finger.

"What's a vet doing wit' a bunch o' pipe wrenches?" he demanded. "And hack saws, yet. Youse ain't planning a jail break?" He grinned widely at the jape.

"Actually, we do a bit of plumbing on the side," O'Leary said. "We're combination animal doctors and plumbers, you see."

"Yeah?" the cop scratched the back of his thick neck. He yawned. "Well, if you can fix old George's plumbing,

Jemimah'll be your friend fer life." He guffawed, cleared his throat, spat, and gave Lom a suspicious look.

"Ain't I see youse before, Pops?"

"Not unless you've been down with an attack of goat fever, Junior," the old man snapped. "And don't call me Pops."

"Well, we'd better be getting along," Lafayette said hastily. "Actually, it was a leaky faucet we were after. In the tower, Roy said. So—"

"Nix, Bub. Nobody goes up inna tower. Off limits, like. Quarantine."

"Yes. Well, Roy's point was that the drip was annoying the patient—"

"What patient? There ain't no patient inna tower. They're all in the Royal Apartment wing."

"The patient fellows on duty there, I was about to say," O'Leary recovered nimbly. "Just imagine pulling four on and four off with a leaky faucet going drip, drip, drip, drip, drip, drip . . ."

"Yeah, yeah—I get the idear. Well—as long as it's fer the boys. I'll send Clarence here along wit' youse." The NCO beckoned to a slack-faced loon with unevenly focused eyes.

"That's all right, Lieutenant, we can find it—" Lafayette started; but the cop cut him off with a curt gesture.

"Nobody don't go inna tower wit'out he got a escort," he stated firmly.

"Well—in that case," O'Leary conceded the point. Clarence pulled on his coat, strapped on his sword, gave O'Leary a vague look and stood waiting.

"You, uh, kind of got to tell Clarence what to do," the NCO said to Lafayette behind his hand. "Like, in detail, if you know what I mean."

"Let's go, Clarence," Lafayette said. "To the tower."

In the courtyard, bright with the late-afternoon sun, Lom overtook O'Leary. "When are we going to dispose of this cretin and make our escape?" he whispered.

"Change of plan," Lafayette murmured. "'Getting Clarence was a big break. With an escort we can go where we want to.'"

"Have you lost your wits? Our only chance is to get clear of this place, and regroup!"

"Let's face it: we'd never get past the gate."

"But—what can you hope to accomplish, skulking about inside the lion's den?"

"Just as I told the gendarmes—the tower—up there." Lafayette pointed to a lofty spire soaring high in the blue sky, a pennant snapping from the flagstaff at its peak.

"Whatever for?" Lom gasped. "We'll be trapped!"

"Classified," Lafayette said.

"Hey," Clarence spoke suddenly in a hoarse whisper. "Hows come we're whispering?"

"It's a secret mission," O'Leary replied. "We're counting on you, Clarence."

"Oh, boy," Clarence said happily. Lom snorted.

Lafayette led the way into the palace proper via a side door—the same door through which he had left that night—only two weeks before, but seeming like a lifetime—for his ill-fated rendezvous with the Red Bull. Inside, he motioned Lom and Clarence along a narrow corridor that passed behind the State Dining Room. Through a half-open door he saw the long tables spread with dazzling linen, adorned with colorful floral centerpieces—a glimpse of another life.

"Looks like they're making ready for a celebration," Lom observed.

"Yeah," Clarence nodded vigorously. "A big blowout scheduled fer tonight. Duh woid is, duh king, he's gonna make a speech, which all duh notables dey'll be dere."

"Keep moving!" Lom hissed. "We'll be seen—and I

doubt if the household major domos will be as readily satisfied with explanations involving medical ministrations to sick pipes at those flatfoots!"

"Hey—dat sounded like it could grow up tuh be a doity crack at us cops," Clarence muttered.

"No offense," Lom reassured him.

They resumed their cautious progress, paused at a brocaded hanging through which Lafayette poked his head to survey the mirrored grand hall. "Come on— the coast is clear."

"Where is everybody?" Lom queried. "The place is like a mausoleum."

"Never mind questioning our good fortune. Let's just take advantage of it."

They reached the back stairs without incident. On the second floor, they passed a red-eyed maidservant with a mop and bucket, who gave them a tearful look and hurried on. Three flights higher a guard lounged on the landing, reading a newspaper with the aid of a blunt forefinger.

"Whazzis?" he inquired, looking suspiciously at the two adventurers. "Who's these mugs, Clarence?"

"Dat's uh like secret," Clarence whispered. "Shhhh."

"Special mission," O'Leary amplified, "under the personal supervision of Sir Lafayette—"

"You mean King Lafayette, don't you, pal?"

"Right. Now his Majesty has his eye on you, corporal—"

"Corporal, my grandma's pickled bananas," the fellow growled. "I been in this outfit nine years and I ain't got stripe one yet."

"You'll have two, as soon as this job is over," O'Leary said. "I personally guarantee it.

"Yeah? Whom did you say you was, sir?"

"A . . . a person in whom his Majesty resides special confidence."

"And where do you think you're going?" the guard inquired as O'Leary started past him.

"Up there." O'Leary pointed.

"Uh-uh," the man planted himself in Lafayette's path.

"Not without a OK from the sergeant, chum."

"Don't you think a king outweighs a sergeant, corporal?"

"Could be—but I work for the sergeant. He works for the lieutenant; *he* works for the captian; *he* works for the colonel—"

"I'm familiar with the intricacies of the military hierarchy," O'Leary napped. "But we don't have time to waste right now going through channels."

"Nobody goes up without a pass," the guard said.

"Will this do?" Lom inquired at O'Leary's elbow. There was a soft *bzapp!* The unfortunate sentry stiffened, staggered two steps, and fell heavily on the purple carpet.

"Tsk. Drunk on duty," Lafayette said. "Make a note of that, Clarence."

They hurried on, Lom puffing hard, Clarence bringing up the rear, around and around the winding staircase. The steps narrowed, steepened between bare stone walls. The climb ended on a small landing before a massive woodplank door.

"Wh-what's this?" Lom panted.

"This is as far as we go—without an understanding," O'Leary said. "Note the lock on the door. I know the combination. You don't."

"So?"

"Give me that trick ball-point, and I'll unlock it."

"Not likely," Lom snapped. "Why should I give a rap whether you unlock it or not?"

"Listen," O'Leary invited. From the stairwell, sounds were rising: sounds of alarm.

"They've found that chap we dealt with down below," Lom said. "We should have hidden him—"

"They'd have noticed he was missing. They'll be here in a minute or two."

"Trapped! You treacher, I should have known better—"

"Shhh! Clarance won't understand," Lafayette said softly as the guardsman arrived, breathing hard. "Anyway, we're not trapped—not if we hide in there." He

142

hooked a thumb at the door.

"What's in there? Why did you lead me into a cul-de-sac—"

"It's Nicodaeus' old lab. He was an Inspector, sent in here by Central to investigate a Probability Stress. It's full of special equipment. We'll find everything we need—"

"Well, for heaven's sake, get it open, man!" Lom cut in as the sounds of ascending feet rang clearly from below.

"First, the zap gun, Lom. Just so you aren't tempted to use it on me."

"And what's to keep *you* from using it on *me*?"

"I won't—unless you make a false move. Make up your mind. We have about thirty seconds."

"Blackmail," Lom muttered, and handed over the weapon.

"Once inside we're home safe," O'Leary said. "Let's see, now. It's been a long time since I used this combination . . ." He twirled the dial; the feet pounding below came closer. The lock snicked and opened. O'Leary pushed the door wide.

"Clarence—inside, quick!"

The harquebusier stepped through hesitantly; Lom ducked after him. O'Leary followed, closed the door and set the lock.

"Full of equipment, eh?" Lom rasped behind him.

He turned; in the dim light filtering down through dusty clerestory windows, Lafayette stared in dismay at blank stone walls and a bare stone floor.

"Stripped!" he groaned.

"Just as I thought," Lom said in a deadly tone. "Betrayal. But I'm afraid you won't live to complete you plans, traitor!" Lafayette turned, was looking down the barrel of a slim, deadly-looking pistol.

"Another of your inventions?" he inquired, backing away.

"Quite correct. I call it a disaster gun, for reasons which you'll, alas, not survive to observe. Say your prayers, my boy. At the count of three, you die."

Outside, boots clumped on the landing. Someone rattled the door.

"Geeze, where could they of went?" a querelous voice inquired.

"Maybe t'rough duh door," another replied.

"Negative, it's locked, and nobody but King Lafayette don't know the combination."

"Nuts, Morton. Let's bust it down—"

"I say negative, Irving! They didn't go that way! You must of give us a bum steer. They never come up here—"

"Where else could they of went? They gotta of went t'rough duh door!"

"They din't!"

"How do you know?"

"They din't because they cun't, rum-dum!"

The door rattled again. "Yeah—I guess yez'r right. Like you said, nobody but King Lafayette could spring dat latch."

The booted feet withdrew.

Lafayette swallowed hard, his eyes on the gun. "Well—what are you waiting for? They're gone. Nobody will hear you killing me. And I deserve whatever happens for being dumb enough to forget to search you."

Lom was frowning thoughtfully. "That fellow said . . . that only King Lafayette knew the combination. That being the case—how did *you* open it—"

"We've been all over that, remember? You didn't believe me."

"You could have shouted whilst the men were outside. It might not have saved your life, but it would have cooked my goose. Yet—you failed to. Why?"

"Maybe I have a goose of my own."

"Hmmm. My boy, I'm inclined to give you one more chance—in spite of your having led me into this dead end.

Just what did you intend to accomplish in this vacant chamber?"

"It shouldn't have been vacant," O'Leary snapped. "That lock is a special Probability Lab model, unpickable. But—somebody picked it." He frowned in deep thought. "I've noticed that there are residual traits that seem to stay with the flesh, even when the minds are switched. As Tazlo Haz, I could almost fly. And I mastered merging, with little concentration." He looked at his hands. "And it would never have occurred to *me* to lift that key from Percy's belt—Zorro's fingers did it on their own. So—the fellow who's wearing my body must have gotten certain skills along with it—including the combination."

"Very well . . ." Lom half-lowered the gun. "Assuming I accept that rather dubious explanation: what do you propose we do now?"

"Are we partners again?"

"Of sorts. By the way, you'd better return the sonic projector."

Lom jumped as Clarance spoke at his elbow: "Hey—you guys gonna chin all day? Let's get duh secret pipes fixed and blow outa here. Duh joint gives me duh willies."

"Don't creep up on me like that!" Lom snapped. "As for you, O'Leary—or whoever you are: you've brought me here—now do something!"

Lafayette looked around the gloomy chamber. The last time he had seen it, the wall cabinets which now gaped empty had been crowded with cryptic gear. The Court Magician's workbench, once littered with alembics and retorts and arcane assemblies, was now a bare slab of stained marble. Above, where the black crackle-finish panel with its ranked dials had been, snarled wires protruded from the bare wall.

"Even the skeleton's gone," he lamented. "It was gilded. It used to hang from a wire in the middle of the room. Very atmospheric."

"Skeletons?" Lom rapped. "What sort of mumbo jumbo is this? You said this fellow Nicodaeus was an Inspec-

145

tor of Continua, working out of Central—"

"Right—the skeleton and the stuffed owls and the bottled eye of newt were just window dressings, in case anybody stumbled in here."

"How did *you* happen to stumble in here? No self-respecting Inspector would allow a local in his operations room."

"I wasn't a local. And he didn't exactly allow me in. I came up here to find out what he knew about Princess Adoranne's disappearance. Frankly, I was ready to slit his weasand, but he talked me out of it."

"Indeed? And how, may I ask? You seem remarkably pertinacious of erroneous theories."

"Your vocabulary gets more portentious all the time," O'Leary said. "He convinced me he was what he said he was—which is more than you've done."

"And how did he accomplish that feat?"

"He made a phone call."

"Oh? I was unaware that telephones were known in this Locus."

"They aren't. Just the one, a hot-line direct to Central. It used to be over there"—O'Leary gestured—"in a cabinet behind the door."

"This is all very nostalgic, I'm sure—but it isn't resolving the present contretemps," Lom said.

"Hey, gents," Clarence called from across the room. "What—"

"Not now, Clarence," O'Leary said. "Look here, Lom, it's not my fault the lab's been cleaned out. And it's not doing us any good to stand here and carp about it. We still have our freedom; what are we going to do with it?"

"You were the mastermind who had everything in hand!" Lom said testily. "What do *you* propose?"

"We have to put our heads together, Lom. What do *you* think we ought to do?"

"Hey, fellas," Clarence spoke up. "What's—"

"Not now, Clarence," Lom said over his shoulder. "Frankly, it looks to me as if we have no choice in the matter. We'll have to simply confront this King Lafayette

146

—this false King Lafayette if your tale is to be credited—and . . . and . . ."

"And what? Invite him to hang us in chains from the palace walls?"

"Blast it, if I could only get my hands on my hands . . ." Lom muttered.

"What's that supposed to mean?"

"Nothing. Forget I said it."

"You've got a thing about hands, haven't you?" O'Leary snarled. "Don't think I haven't seen you playing with your fingers when you thought I wasn't looking."

"I wasn't playing, you impertinent upstart! I was . . . oh, never mind."

"Go ahead," O'Leary said, and slumped against the wall. "You might as well snap your lid in your own way. Lets' face it: we're at the end of our tether."

Lom laughed hollowly. "You know—I'm almost convinced, at last, that you're what you say your are. What a pity it's too late to do any good."

"Hey," Clarence said. "Pardon duh innerruption—but what's dis funny-looking contraption, which I found it inna cupboard behind duh door?"

Lafayette looked dully toward the man. He went rigid.

"The telephone!" he yelled. "Don't drop it, Clarence!"


5


"Clarence, my lad, you're a genuis," Lom chortled, hurrying forward. "Here, just hand me that—"

"Not on your life," O'Leary said, and elbowed the old man aside to grab the old-fashioned, brass-trimmed instrument from Clarence. "Anyway, I'm the only one who knows the number!" He held the receiver to his ear, jiggled the hook.

"Hello? Hello, Central—"

There was a sharp *ping!* and a hum that went on and on.

"Come on! Answer!" Lafayette enjoined.

"Central," a tinny voice said brightly in his ear. "Number, please."

"It's—let's see . . . nine, five, three . . . four, nine, oh . . . oh, two, one-one."

"That is a restricted number, sir. Kindly refer to your directory for an alternate—"

"I don't have a directory! Please! This is an emergency!"

"Well—I'll speak to my supervisor. Hold the line, please."

"What do they say?" Lom asked breathlessly.

"She's speaking to her supervisor."

"What about?"

"I don't know—"

"Here—give me that telephone!" Lom made a grab; Lafayette bumbled the instrument, bobbled it, missed as Lom plunged for it. Clarence made a brilliant save an inch from the floor as the two staggered back in an off-balance embrace.

"Uh, no'm, it ain't," Clarence was saying into the mouthpiece as Lafayette extricated himself. "Name of Clarence: K . . . L . . . A . . . I . . . N . . . T . . . S . . ." He gave O'Leary an aggrieved look as the latter snatched the phone away.

"Yes? To whom did you wish to speak, sir?" a brisk voice said.

"Inspector Nicodaeus—only I understand he's on a field job somewhere—so just give me whoever's taking his place! I have vital information to report!"

"From where are you calling, sir?"

"Artesia—but never mnid that—just give me somebody who can do something about—"

"Hold the line, please."

"Wait a minute! Hello! Hello?"

"What do they say?" Lom demanded.

"Nothing. I'm holding the line."

"O'Leary—if you lose that connection—"

"I know; it might be fifty years before I get through again."

"Ah, there, O'Leary?" a hearty voice came on the line. "Good to hear from you. All's now well, I take it?"

"Well? Are you kidding? It couldn't be worse! Adoranne and Alain are dying of some unknown disease, there's a phony king going around kicking cats, and I'm trapped in the tower!"

"Here, who is this? I know O'Leary's voice, and this isn't it!"

"I've been all over that! I'm temporarily a fellow named Zorro, but actually I'm O'Leary, only somebody else is me, and he's running amok, and—"

"Look here, whoever you are—unauthorized use of the Central Comm Net is an offense punishable by fine, brainscrape, and imprisonment, or any combination thereof! Now, get off the line, and—"

"You're not listening! I'm in trouble! Artesia's in trouble! We need help!"

"I'm sure," the strange voice said icily, "that matters are now well in hand. You needn't trouble yourself further—"

"Trouble myself—are you out of your hairpiece? If those trigger-happy guards get their hands on me, it'll be the firing squad!"

"See here, fellow: just take your grievances to the agent on the scene. If you have a legitimate case, it will be looked into. Now—"

"Agent? What agent? I'm the Central agent here, and I've been faked out of position and—"

"The regular man, Mr. O'Leary, is incapacitated, it appears. However, a Special Field Agent was dispatched to the Locus some hours ago, with instructions to proceed direct to the palace and make contact with one Princess Adoranne. That being the case—"

"You've sent a special agent in? Here? To Artesia?"

"That's what I said," the voice snapped. "Now if you'll excuse me—"

"Where is he? How will I recognize him? What—"

There was a sharp click, and the wavering hum of a dead line. Lafayette jiggled and yelled, but to no avail.

"Well? Well?" Lom was fairly dancing with impatience.

"He hung up on me. But I managed to pry some good news out of him: they've sent another agent in, probably one of their best men, with full powers. He'll have things straightened out in a hurry."

"Oh? Indeed. I see. Ha-hum."

"You don't seem overjoyed."

Lom pulled at his lower lip, frowning intently. "Actually," he said, "I'm not at all sure this is a desirable development at just this point."

"What's *that* remark supposed to mean?"

"Our antagonist, my boy, is a man of fiendish cleverness. At this moment he holds all the cards. Against him, a lone Agent hasn't a chance."

"Nonsense. I admit the fellow may not know the score—having me not be me is a bit confusing. But all I have to do is make contact with this new Agent, fill him in on a few facts, and make the pinch—"

"But that may not be so easy. Remember: I have one vital datum that you lack."

"Oh? What's that?"

"I," said Lom, "know who the villain is."

# CHAPTER TEN

## 1

"You could have saved some time," Lafayette said, "if you'd mentioned this a little earlier."

"How could I? I thought you were his partner in the scheme."

"All right—who is he? Zorro?"

"Good heavens, no—"

"Not the Red Bull?"

"Nothing like that. You've never met him. The fact is, he's a renegade Commissioner of the Central Authority, by the name of Quelius."

"A commissioner? Ye gods—one of the top men—"

"Precisely. Now you can see the seriousness ·of his defection. I was his first victim. Then you. Now he's gobbling up an entire kingdom—and it will require a good deal more than honest intentions to topple the madman."

"All right—what's your suggestion?"

"First, we must make contact with this new chap Central's sent in, before he comes to grief. Presumably he's here in the palace by now, possibly in disguise. We'll attempt to intercept him when he calls on the princess."

"How are we going to recognize him?"

"I have," Lom said, patting his pockets, "a small ID device. When within fifty feet of a Central Authority ID card, it emits a warning buzz. Its failure to react to you was one of the principal reasons for my suspicions of you."

"Ummp. My ID is in a dresser drawer, downstairs."

"Quite. Now, at this point I suggest we divide forces. In that way, if one of us is caught the other may still get by in the confusion."

"Ummm. Shall we flip a coin?"

"I'll go first, dear boy. Now—what is the most direct route to the royal apartments?"

Lafayette told him. "Be careful," he finished. "There'll be guards six deep around the whole wing."

"Never fear, I shall make judicious use of the sonic projector. And I suppose you may as well have the disaster gun. But I'd suggest using it only in emergency. It's never been tested, you know."

"Thanks a lot." O'Leary accepted the weapon gingerly.

"Well—no point in waiting. I suppose. You follow in, oh, ten minutes, eh?" Lom moved to the door.

"Wait a minute," Lafayette said. "You've got your buzzer to identify the agent—but what do *I* use?"

"I should think any stranger might be a likely prospect. Ta-ta, my lad. I'll see you in court." The old fellow opened the door and slipped out. Lafayette listened. Two minutes passed with no audible alarm.

"So far so good," Lafayette murmured. "Now it's my turn."

Clarence was sound asleep, sitting in a corner with his head tilted on one shoulder. He opened his eyes, blinking in a bewildered way when Lafayette tapped him on the knee.

"I'm going now, Clarence. You can go back to the squad room. If anybody asks, tell them we went home. And thanks a lot."

"Geeze," Clarence said, rubbing his eyes. He yawned prodigiously. "I wanna stay on duh job, boss. Dis cloak and dagger game is loads o' fun."

"Sure—but we need you back with the troops—someone who knows the score in case things go wrong."

"Yeah! Wow! Duh fellers won't never know I'm on a secret lay, which I'm woiking as usual wit' every appearance o' normality, an' all."

"That's the idea—" Lafayette jumped fourteen inches as a sharp ring sounded from the cabinet beside the door.

"Hey—dat sounds like duh doorbell," Clarence said. "OK if I answer it, boss?"

"It's the phone," O'Leary said, and grabbed it up. "Hello?"

"Oh, is that you?" It was the same voice he had last spoken to. "I say, look here, it appears something has come up; a Very Important Person wishes a word with you. Just hang on."

There was an electrical clatter, and a new voice spoke:

"Hello? This is Inspector Nicodaeus. To whom am I speaking, please?"

"Nicodaeus! Am I glad to hear from you! When did you get back?"

"Kindly identify yourself!"

"Identify myself? Oh, you mean because of the voice. Don't let that bother you—it's Lafayette. Just think of me as a little hoarse—"

"A little *what?* Look here, they told me there was a chap claiming to be O'Leary in another form, but nothing was said about *this!*"

"My voice," O'Leary said, striving for calm. "Not me. Listen, Nicodaeus—there's a serious emergency here in Artesia—"

"One moment," interrupted the voice on the line. "Tell me: what were the first words you ever said to me—assuming you are, as you claim, Sir Lafayette?"

"Look, is this necessary—"

"It is," Nicodaeus said in a tone of finality.

"Well—ah—I think you asked me where I was from, and I told you."

"Eh? Hmmm. Maybe you're right. I was thinking—but never mind. Now then: what was the object I showed you which first aroused your suspicions that I might be more

153

than a mere Court Magician?"

"Let see. A . . . a Ronson lighter?"

"By Jove, I believe you're right! Is that really you, Lafayette?"

"Of course! Let's stop wasting time! How soon can you have a couple of platoons of Special Field Agents in here to arrest this imposter who's rampaging around kicking cats and sleeping in my bed?"

"That's what I'm calling about, Lafayette. When I heard someone representing himself as you had been here at Central, I immediately looked into the situation—and what I've turned up isn't good—"

"I already knew that! The question is—"

"The question is more complicated than you know, Lafayette. Have you ever heard of a man named Quelius?"

"Quelius? Commissioner Quelius?"

"The same. Well, it seems that Quelius has run amok. He was Chief of Research, you know—"

"No, I didn't know—but I've already heard about him. Glad you confirmed what my friend Lom told me about him. But can't this discussion wait until after we've cleaned up this mess?"

"That's what I'm trying to tell you, Lafayette! Quelius, it now appears, has absconded with the entire contents of the Top Cosmic Lab, including our top researcher, Jorlemagne. From bits and pieces of evidence, we've learned that he has perfectd a device with which he plans to seal off the Artesia continuum from any further contact with Central—to shift the entire Locus, in effect, into a new alignment, rendering himself forever safe from apprehension—and placing Artesia forever under his domination!"

"I never heard of any such gadget! That's impossible!"

"Not at all; in fact, it's quite easy, it appears, once given the basic theory. You remember a device called a Suppressor?"

"How could I forget? If it hadn't been for that, I

154

wouldn't be in the fix I'm in now! How about lifting it, so I can go into action?"

"I'm afraid that's already been taken out of our hands," Nicodaeus said grimly. "Phase one of Quelius' plan has already gone into effect. The first step was to erect a Suppressor barrier around the entire Locus, cutting off all physical contact. This went into action only minutes ago. Our sole link is now this telephone connection—"

"You mean—you can't send any more men in?"

"Or out. Now it's up to you, Lafayette. Somehow, you must locate this man Quelius and lay him by the heels before his second phase is activated and Artesia is cut off forever!"

"How . . . how much time have I got?"

"Not much, I fear. Minutes, perhaps; hours at best. I suggest you go into action with all haste. I needn't remind you what's at stake!"

"And there's *nothing* Central can do to help?"

"Candidly, Lafayette—if more than a single obscure Locus were involved—if there were an actual threat to Central—certain extraordinary measures *might* be taken. But as it is, only my personal, sentimental interest in Artesia caused me to attempt this call. The simplest solution for Central, you must understand, is to let the matter solve itself. No doubt that's precisely the policy on which Quelius is counting for immunity. Well, perhaps we'll surprise him."

"Me—single handed—plus one Field Agent you're apparently ready to abandon? What can we do?"

"I'm afraid that's up to you, Lafayette, Nicodaeus said, his voice fainter now as the crackling on the line increased. "I have great confidence in you, you know."

"What does this Quelius look like?" Lafayette shouted.

"He's an elderly man—about five three—bald as an egg."

"Did you say five three, elderly—and bald as an egg?"

"Correct. Not very formidable in appearance, but a deadly antagonist—"

"With a squeaky voice?"

"Why—yes! Have you seen him?"

"Oh, yes, I've seen him," Lafayette said, and uttered a hollow laugh. "I got him into the palace, past the guards, his him until they were gone, gave him explicit directions for reaching Adoranne's apartment, patted him on the head, and sent him on his way . . ."

". . . fayette—what's that . . . hear you . . . fading . . ." The static rose to drown the faint voice.

"Chee, boss, what's duh matter?" Clarence inquired as O'Leary hung up the phone. "Youse are as white as a tombstone!"

"Under the circumstances, that's an apt simile." Lafayette chewed his lower lip, thinking hard. Lom—or Quelius—at least hadn't lied when he named the villain of the piece—had used him like a paper towel. He'd gotten himself thrown in the same dungeon, pumped him dry of information, and then removed himself to a place of safety, leaving a gullible O'Leary to fare forth into the waiting arms of the enemy.

"Well, I'll fool him on that point, anyway," O'Leary said aloud. "Clarence—how would you like to have a *real* undercover assignment?"

"Chee, boss! Great!"

"All right, listen carefully. . . ."

2

"Wait five minutes," O'Leary completed his instructions. "Then go into action. And remember: stick to your story, no matter what—until I give you the signal."

"Got it, Chief."

"Well—so long, and good luck." Lafayette opened the double glass doors that led onto the small balcony, stepped out into a drizzling rain under a sky the color of aged pewter.

"Splendid," he commented. "It fits right in with the

overall picture." The iron railing was cold and slippery under his hands as he climbed over, lowered himself to find a foothold in the dense growth of vines below.

"Hey," Clarence said, leaning over to stare down at him. "A guy could like get hurt iff'n he was to fall offa dere."

"I've made this climb before," O'Leary reassured him. "In the dark. Now go back inside before you catch cold." He started down, wet leaves slapping at his face, icy water running down inside his sleeves. By the time he reached the stone coping twenty feet below, he was soaking wet. Carefully not looking down at the paved court a hundred feet beneath him, he made his way around the tower to a point above the slanting, copper-shingled roof of the residential wing. It was another fifteen-foot climb down to a point where he could plant a foot on the gable, which looked far steeper and more slippery than he had remembered.

*No time now for seconds thoughts*, he told himself firmly, and leaped, throwing himself flat. His hands scrabbled at the wet surface; he slid down until his feet went over the edge, his shins, his knees—and stopped.

*All right, heart; slow down.* The heavy copper gutter was under his belt buckle. He hitched himself sideways to a point which he estimated was approximately opposite the window to a small storeroom, then lowered himself over the edge. The window was there, directly before him, three feet away under the overhanging eave. Lafayette swung a toe at the latch securing the shutters; they sprang open, banging in the wind. A second kick, lightly administered, shattered the glass. He tapped with his boot, clearing the shards away.

"All right, O'Leary," he whispered, eying the dark opening. "Here's where that book you read on acrobatics will come in handy."

He swung himself forward, back, forward, back—

On the forward swing he let go, shot feetfirst through the window to slam the floor of the room rump-first.

"Nothing broken," O'Leary concluded after struggling to his feet and hobbling a few steps. He paused to listen to absolute silence. "No alarm. So far so good." He opened the hall door an inch; the passage was empty; not even the usual ceremonial sentries were on duty at the far end. Lafayette slipped out, moved silently along to the gilt and white door to the suite formerly occupied by a favorite courtier of Goruble's. There were no sounds from inside. He tried the latch; it opened and he stepped inside, closing the door behind him

The room was obviously unused now; dust covers were draped over the furniture; the drapes were drawn, the window shuttered. Lafayette went to the far wall, tapped the oak panels, pressed at the precise point in the upper left-hand corner that Yockabump had pointed out to him, long ago. The panel swung inward with a faint squeak, and O'Leary stepped through into the musty passage.

"This is one ace Lom didn't know I was holding," he congratulated himself. "Now, if I can get to Adoranne before *he* does . . ."

It was a difficult fifteen-minute trip through the roughly mortared secret passage system, up narrow ladders, under low-clearance beams, which O'Leary located with his skull, to the black wall behind which lay the royal apartment. Lafayette listened, heard nothing. At his touch the inconspicuous latch clicked open and the panel slid smoothly aside.

Across the deep pile rug he could see the corner of Adoranne's big, canopied four-poster bed. No one was visible in the room. He stepped out—and whirled at the sudden whistle of steel clearing a sheath. A sharp point prodded his throat, and he was looking down the length of a sword blade into the square-jawed and hostile face of Count Alain.

"Hold it, Alain!" O'Leary said with some difficulty, owing to the angle at which his head was tilted. "I'm friendly."

"You have a curious manner of approach for one who means no ill, rascal!" Alain said. "Who are you? What would ye here?"

"I think I'd better let my identity ride for the moment; it would only complicate matters. Just think of me as a friend of Yockabump. He showed me the route here."

"Yockabump? What mare's tail's this? He lies in the palace dungeons, banished there by the madness of the usurper."

"Yes. Well, as it happens, I just escaped from the dungeon myself. Ah—would you mind putting the sword down, Alain? You'll break the skin."

"Aye—and a few bones beside! Speak, varlet! Who sent you here? What's your errand? Assassination, I doubt not!"

"Nonsense! I'm on your side, get it?"

A door across the room opened; a slim figure with golden hair and immense blue eyes appeared, clad in a flowing sky-blue gown.

"Adoranne—tell this clown to put the sword down before he gets into trouble with it," O'Leary called.

"Alain—who—"

"A would-be assassin," Alain growled.

"A friend of Yockabump; I came to help!" O'Leary countered.

"Alain—lower your blade. Let's hear what the poor man has to say."

"Well, then: speak. But at the first false move . . ." Alain stepped back and lowered the sword. O'Leary fingered his throat and let out a long breath.

"Listen," he said. "There's no time for formalities. I'm glad to see you two in good shape. The story is you're dying of a mysterious fever—"

"Aye, 'tis the lie spread by that treacher I once named as friend," Alain rumbled.

"There's a fellow on his way here—a man named Quelius, alias Lom." Lafayette described his former ally. "Have you seen him?"

Both Alain and Adoranne shook their heads.

"Good. He's the one who's at the bottom of this whole fiasco. Now, suppose you kids start by filling me in on the picture from your end?"

"Fellow, you're overfamiliar—" Alain started; but Adoranne put a hand on his arm.

"Hush," she said softly. "As you wish, friend of Yockabump. We, as you see, are held prisoner in our own apartments. His Majesty assures us that it's but a temporary measure—"

"Majesty, my left elbow!" Alain cut in. "I knew the first time I laid eyes on the miscreant no good would come of him! King Lafayette indeed! Wait 'til I lay hands on the treacher's neck!"

"As I remember, you didn't do so well the last time you two had a run-in," O'Leary observed. "Anyway, maybe you ought to make a few allowances. Maybe it's not really Lafayette O'Leary at all, who from all reports is a prince of a fellow, and—"

"Think you not I know the oil-tongued wretch who once forced his way into Her Highness's good graces with his trickery, and—"

"Trickery! That was no trick, just superior personal magnetism. And killing Lod was a pretty hard thing even for you to brush off as sleight-of-hand—and how about killing the dragon? I suppose you could have done better?"

"Enough, sirrah!" Adoranne cut in. "Alain—stay to the subject."

"All right. So this blackguard, having lulled us into a

false sense of security by lying low for a time, suddenly revealed his true colors. First, he came to her Highness with tales of an invading army. When, at my advice, she asked for evidence, he put us off with lies, meantime assuming what he termed emergency powers—which her Highness had not authorized. When I complained—we found ourselves one morning locked in, under guard by coarse fellows, new recruited, in the pay of O'Leary. When next we had tidings, whispered through a keyhole by a loyal housemaid, the scoundrel had in sooth declared himself to be regent!"

"All right—it's about as bad as it could be," O'Leary said. "Now, there are angles to this that I can't explain right now—you wouldn't believe me if I did—but what it boils down to is that we have to nail this fellow Quelius. He's the real power behind the throne. The imposter who's claiming to be O'Leary is working for him—"

" 'Tis no imposter, but O'Leary's self!" Alain rasped.

"What makes you so sure? Did Lafayette O'Leary ever do anything before to make you doubt him? Hasn't he always been true-blue, loyal, brave, honest—"

"I never trusted the varlet," Alain said flatly. "His present demeanor but confirms my reservations."

"Speaking of confirmed reservations, we'd better travel," Lafayette snapped. "I can see there's no point in trying to explain anything to you, you fair-weather chum."

"Mind your tongue, lackwit, else I'll probe for your jugular with my point!"

"Yeah, sure. All right, let's stop wasting time. You two can make your escape via the secret passages. I'll wait here for Quelius to show. When he does I'll give him a shot from his own shooter." He patted the disaster gun in his belt.

"What? You think I'd flee and leave even a scurvy knave like you to face the foe alone? Hah! Adoranne, you go, and—"

"Don't prattle nonsense," the princess cut him off coolly. "I stay, of course."

"If this were an ordinary situation, I'd argue with you," Lafayette said. "But under the circumstances, you may as well. If I miss, it's all over for Artesia."

"How is't, sirrah, that you seem to be privy to information unknown to the general public—or even to her Highness?" Alain demanded..

"I'll explain all that later—if there *is* a later."

"Not so," Alain barked. "Who else but a lackey of the tyrant would know his plans?" The sword leaped out to prod O'Leary's chest.

"If you must know, I got the information from a place called Central!"

Alain and Adoranne looked at each other.

"Indeed?" the count murmured. "That being the case, I suppose you'd be pleased to meet a fellow minion of this Central you speak of?"

"Certainly—but you're not supposed to know anything about Central. It's existence is a secret from everybody but accredited Central agents."

"Even so," Alain said. "And it happens, an emissary from Central arrived before you."

"That's right! I'd forgotten! Where is he?"

"Lying down in the next room. Adoranne—wilt summon the agent?"

The princess left the room. Lafayette heard low voices, then soft footfalls on the carpet. A slim, girlish figure in a trim gray uniform appeared in the doorway.

"Daphne!" Lafayette gasped. "What are *you* doing here?"

5

"You know her?" Alain said in an amazed tone.

"I thought you were safe at Central casting," Lafayette said, starting forward. "You poor kid, I knew they'd sent

162

someone, but it never occurred to me they'd be idiots enough to—"

Daphne jerked a pistol from the holster at her waist, aimed it at O'Leary.

"I don't know how you know my name," she said in a voice with only the faintest quaver, "but if you take another step, I'll fire!"

"Daphne—it's me—Lafayette! Don't you know me?"

"What, you, too? Does everybody think I'm so addled I don't know my own husband?"

Lafayette moistened his lips and took a deep breath. "Look, Daphne—try to understand. I don't look like myself, I know. I look like a Wayfarer named Zorro. But actually I'm me, you see?"

"I see you're out of your mind! Stand back!"

"Daphne—listen to me! I stepped out that night —Wednesday, I think it was, two weeks ago—to, er, drop down to the A & D—and *this* happened to me! It's all because of a thing called a Focal Referent. A fellow named Quelius is responsible. He paid the Red Bull to entice me down there, and—"

"Stop it! You're not Lafayette! He's tall, and handsome, in a baby-faced sort of way, and he has curly hair and the sweetest smile, especially when he's done something foolish—"

"Like this!" Lafayette smiled his most sheepish smile. "See?" He said between his teeth. Daphne yipped and jumped back.

"Not anything like that, you oily, leering, monster!"

"Look, Zorro can't help it if he has close-set eyes!"

"Enough of this, varlet!" Alain roared. "Art daft, lout? Think you and the Countess Daphne—and Her Highness and myself as well—know not this turncoat O'Leary on sight?"

"He's not a turncoat!" Daphne cried, whirling on Alain. "He's just . . . just . . . sick . . . or something." She sniffled suddenly, and blinked back a tear.

"Look, we can't have a falling-out now over a little mis-

163

understanding," Lafayette appealed. "Forget my identity; the important thing is that we stop Quelius—fast! He's got some sort of probability engine set up that will rotate Artesia right out of the Continuum! Once he does that, he's safe forever from outside interference from Central!"

"What do *you* know about Central?"

"Don't you remember? You saw me there, yesterday! You even helped me—"

"I saw another crazy man there who tried to convince me he was Lafayette O'Leary. I never saw you before in my life—or him, either!"

"Daphne—they were both me! I mean, I was both of them! I mean—oh, never mind. The point is—I'm on your side—and Adoranne's side. I just talked to Nicodaeus. He was the one who warned me about Lom—I mean Quelius!"

"Do you have any proof?"

'Wel—nothing documentary—but Daphne—listen: close your eyes, and imagine I've got a bad cold, or got hit in the larynx by a polo ball, or something. Now . . . remember the night I met you? You were wearing nothing but soapsuds, remember? So I ordered up a nice dress for you to wear to the ball—a pink and silver one. And later that evening you saved my life for the first time by dropping the chamber pot on Count Alain's head! And—"

"Who told you all this!"

"Nobody! It's me, I remember it! Just pretend I'm . . . I'm enchanted or something, like the frog prince. Inside this unwashed exterior is the same old Lafayette who wooed you and won you!"

"There *is* something . . . it's almost as if . . ."

"Then you do recognize me?"

"No! But . . . but I suppose there's no harm in listening to what you have to say—even if you *are* crazy."

"Well, that's something . . ."

"We've heard enough madman's raving," Alain said. "The question remains—what to do? We know the false king plans some great coup for this evening; the rumors make that plain. We must make our move before then—or not at all. I say the time has come for me to fare forth, beat my way through the usurper's hirelings who guard us here, and slay their master as he takes his place in the banquet hall!"

"You'd never make it, Al," O'Leary said flatly. "Anyway, there's no need for a grandstand play. We can use the secret passages and pop up in the ballroom, surprise, surprise."

"If we can trust this intelligence of hidden ways . . ."

"Alain—he's our friend; I feel it. It almost seems I know him . . ." Adoranne looked searchingly at O'Leary.

He sighed. "Let's not get me started on that again," he said. "What time is this big affair scheduled for?"

"Eight p.m.—about an hour from now."

"Unless I'm badly mistaken, you'll have callers before then—bound on the errand you thought I was on. Quelius can't afford to have you alive when his puppet springs his big announcement this evening. He probably figures on the confusion of the big dance to cover sneaking the bodies out of the palace. Later he'll make the sad announcement that you've fallen victims to the fever. Your showing up in good health will blow that plan off the map. After that we'll have to play it by ear."

"Once in the ballroom, in full sight of the people," Alain mused, "we'll be safe—for the moment. He'd not dare to cut us down before our subjects."

"And our very presence there," Adoranne added, "will give the lie to his claims of our indisposition."

Alain smacked a fist into his palm.

" 'Tis possible—but if this secret way leads into a trap . . ." Alain gave Lafayette a fierce look. "I know who will be first to die."

"Don't be nervous, Al—you'll get through all right," O'Leary assured him. "Now, I think you both ought to look your best, to properly impress the public. Medals, orders, jewels, tiaras—the works."

"You could do with a wash yourself, fellow," Alain addressed O'Leary. "There's a distinct odor of goat about you."

"A bath?" Lafayette said wonderingly. "I'd forgotten such things existed."

"In there." Alain motioned along a short passage toward a door through which were visible pale-green tiles and golden fittings. "And you may burn those garish rags; I think my footman's attire will fit you well enough."

"I guess I can spare the time," Lafayette said, heading for the bathroom.

For a quarter of an hour O'Leary luxuriated in hot, scented water, scrubbing his skin with violet soap until it tingled.

"Easy, boy," he advised himself. "You'll wash all the hide off. Some of that dark shade is permanent. . . ."

Afterward, he shaved, deciding to retain Zorro's mustache, trimmed drastically to an Errol Flynn effect with a pair of fingernail scissors, which he also employed on his fingernails. His glossy blue-black hair was also trimmed lightly and toweled dry, after which, with a minimum of brushing, it fell into a rather dashing natural coif.

Alain had laid out clothing in the anteroom. Lafayette put on clean underwear, tight black pants, a white shirt with baggy sleeves and an open collar. Before adding the black coat provided, he donned the scarlet cummerbund from his former outfit—a recent acquisition, apparently, almost unsoiled. Of necessity he also retained the gold rings on his fingers, as well as the one in his left ear, since they seemed to be permanently attached.

He strolled back along the passage into the drawing room; Daphne turned with a startled expression.

"Oh—it's you. You look different."

"Where are Adoranne and Alain?"

"In their boudoir, dressing."

"You look pretty cute in that uniform, Daphne," O'Leary said. "But I liked you better in soapsuds."

"Please—spare me these fanciful reminiscences, sir! I have no choice but to work with you. But it's silly for

166

somebody who doesn't have the remotest resemblance to Lafayette to attempt to impersonate him!"

"Well—I guess I'll have to settle for a platonic relationship. But it's hard, Daphne. You'll never know how I've missed you these past two weeks, how I've wanted to take you in my arms, and—"

"Don't be impertinent," Daphne said mildly. "You'd best fill me in on the plan."

"Oh, the plan. Well, frankly, the plan needs work. Daphne, did you know you have the most beautiful eyes in the world?"

"Do you really think so? But never mind that. We must talk of what we'll do when we reach the ballroom."

"Well, this fellow Quelius is a potent operator. Our only chance is to sneak up on him and nail him before he can use his sonic projector. Do you know, your hair is like spun onyx. And even in that uniform, your figure is enough to break a man's heart at a hundred yards."

"Silly boy," Daphne murmured. "I must say you look better with a shave. But we really can't stand here chattering all day . . ." She looked up into Lafayette's face as he came up to her. His arms went around her. She sighed and closed her eyes, her lips upturned . . .

"Hey! What are you doing!" he said suddenly. "Kissing a stranger, eh? I'm surprised at you, Daphne!"

She stiffened, then stepped back and swung an openhanded slap that sent him staggering.

"Here—what's this?" Alain spoke up from behind O'Leary. He stood in the doorway, resplendent in a dashing costume of blue and scarlet.

"It's quite all right," Daphne said haughtily, turning her back on O'Leary. "I've dealt with the matter."

Alain gave O'Leary a crooked smile. "The lady is abominably true to her marriage vows," he commented, rubbing his cheek reminiscently.

Adoranne appeared, regal as a fairy queen in silver gown and diamonds. She turned from Alain to O'Leary to Daphne, standing at the window with her back to the room. She went to her, put an arm around her waist.

"Never mind, Daph," she whispered. "I know someday Lafayette will come to his senses."

Daphne sobbed once, dabbed at her eyes, then turned, straight-backed. At that moment there was a peremptory knock at the outer door.

"I think it's time to go," she said.

# CHAPTER ELEVEN

## 1

Ten minutes later they were crowded in the stuffy chamber scarcely a yard deep, ten feet long, concealed in the thickness of the wall behind the ballroom.

"Now, remember," Lafayette said. "Adoranne, you and Alain give me time to get in position. Then wait until this phony's just about to make his big announcement—then spring it on him. Just behave as if everything were normal: this is just a delightful surprise, you recovered unexpectedly, and here you are to join the fun. He'll have to play up to it. And while he's busy trying to regroup, I'll have my chance to take a crack at him."

"But—that will be dangerous for you!" Daphne said. "Why don't we draw lots—or something?"

"He knows all of you; I'll be a stranger to him, a nobody. He won't be watching me."

"He's right, girl," Alain muttered. "But I'll stand ready to join in as opportunity offers."

"All right—here I go." Lafayette pressed the latch, the panel rolled aside, and he slipped through into the dazzle of light and the babble of conversation. The football-field-sized white marble floor was crowded with guests in laces and satins, gold braid and glittering jewels, aglow in the polychrome light from the great chandeliers suspended from the gold-ribbed vault of the high ceiling.

Solemn-looking guards in uniforms with unfamiliar armbands were posted at twenty-foot intervals against the brocaded walls, he noted. By sheer luck he had emerged midway between two of them. A few familiar faces turned casually to glance his way; but most of those present kept their eyes fixed firmly on the great golden chair set up at the far end of the room. And in spite of the superficial appearance of casual gaiety, there was an air of tension, a note of anxiety in the laughter and chatter.

Lafayette moved along the fringes of the crowd unchallenged. He took a drink from a passing tray and downed it at a gulp.

Abruptly, horns sounded. Silence fell, broken by a few nervous coughs. The wide doors at the opposite end of the room swung wide. A second fanfare blared. Then a tall, slender, fair-haired man appeared, strolling through the archway with an air of negligent authority. He was dressed in yellow silks adorned with white ermine, and a light-weight sport-model crown was cocked at a jaunty angle on his head.

"Why, the poor stumble-bum looks like a complete nincompoop!" O'Leary muttered aloud. "Doesn't he know yellow takes all the color out of my complexion?"

"Shhh!" hissed a stout nobleman in purple at Lafayette's elbow. "His spies are everywhere!"

"Listen," O'Leary said urgently. "That popinjay isn't the real—"

"Oh, I know, I know! Hold your tongue, sir! Do you want to get us all hanged?" The man in purple moved off quickly.

The regent sauntered across to the dais, stepped up assisted by a cluster of courtiers, and seated himself grandly in the ornate chair. He tucked one foot back, thrust out the other, and leaned forward, resting his chin on one fist.

"Ha! Just like Henry the Eighth in a grade-B movie," O'Leary murmured, netting several apprehensive looks from those about him. As he made his way closer a func-

170

tionary—a former second assistant stock room tallier, Lafayette saw, now decked out in full ceremonial garb—stepped forward, cleared his throat, unrolled a scroll with a flourish.

"Milords and ladies, his Royal Highness, Prince Lafayette, will graciously address the assemblage," he piped in a thin voice.

There was a patter of applause. The man in the golden chair shifted his chin to the other fist.

"Loyal subjects," he said in a mellow tenor, "how I admire your brave spirits—your undaunted gallantry in joining me here this evening—defying gloom, rejecting the melancholy counsels of those who would have us quail before the grim specter now hovering over our beloved Princess and her esteemed consort. If they could join us this evening, they would be the first to applaud you, carrying on in the gala mood they loved—love, that is—so well." The regent paused to shift position again.

"Look at that dumbbell, trying ot talk with his jaw on his fist," Lafayette whispered to no one in particular. "He looks like a terminal paresis case."

Several people moved away from him; but one wizened little fellow in scarlet velvet muttered, "Hear! Hear!"

"Why is everybody standing around listening to this clown?" Lafayette asked the old gentleman. "Why don't they do something?"

"Eh? You ask a question like that? Have you forgotten Sir Lafayette's many services to the crown—and the squads of armed bravos he's lately hired to help secure his continued popularity, the while he so unselfishly volunteers his services during our ruler's indisposition?"

"Lord Archibald—what would you say if I said Adoranne's not really sick at all?" Lafayette inquired, *sotto voce*.

"Say? Why, I'd say you were prey to wishful thinking. And have we met, sir?"

"No—not exactly. But if she *were* actually well—just being held incommunicado—"

"Then all the cut-necks in Hell wouldn't restrain any sword from her service, sir!"

"Shhh! Good by, Lord Archie—and keep your eyes peeled." O'Leary moved off as the regent droned on, took up a position some ten yards from the speaker, in the front rank of the crowd.

". . . it is therefore incumbent on me—a realization to which I come with inexpressible reluctance—to formally assume a title commensurate with the dignities residing in the *de facto* Chief of the Artesian state. Accordingly—and with a heavy heart—" The regent broke off as his eye fell on O'Leary. For a long moment he gazed blankly at him. Suddenly he jerked upright, his eyes blazing, pointed a finger at O'Leary.

"Seize me that traitor!" he roared.

## 2

There were small shrieks and muttered exclamations as a squad of strong-arm men jostled their way through the press to grab Lafayette by both arms and the back of the neck. He landed one solid kick to a uniformed kneecap before a double wrist lock immobilized him.

"Don't kill him yet!" the regent yelled; then, as startled faces jerked around to stare at him, he managed an undernourished smile. "I mean to say, remember the prisoner's constitutional rights, lads, and treat him with all due gentility."

"What's the charge?" O'Leary croaked, speaking with difficulty because of the awkward angle at which his chin was being crushed against his sternum.

"Take him away," the regent snapped. "I'll question him later."

"One moment, if you please, sir!" a cracked voice piped up. Lord Archibald pushed his way forward to stand before the golden chair.

"I, too, would like to know the nature of the charge," he said.

"What's this? You dare to question me—that is, ah, why, my dear Archie—suppose we discuss the matter latter—in private. Security of the realm involved and all that—"

"Sire, the security of the realm is involved at any time that one of her citizens is arrested arbitrarily!"

There was a small murmur of assent that faded swiftly as the man in the chair thrust out his lower lip and frowned down at the crowd.

"I perceive," he said in a lowering tone, "that the time has come for the enforcement of more stringent wartime regulations regarding free speech—or more properly—treason!"

"Treason against what, Messire?" Archibald persisted.

"Against me, your sovereign!"

"Princess Adoranne, sire, is *my* sovereign!" the old nobleman said loudly.

"I may as well tell you—your Princess is dead!"

There was an instant, dead silence. And in the silence, a clear feminine voice spoke:

"Liar!"

All heads whirled; Adoranne, radiant in silver and pearls, her long hair floating like a golden fog behind her, advanced through an aisle that opened magically before her. Behind her, Count Alain strode, tall and impressively handsome in tailcoat and spurs. Daphne followed, trim and beautiful, her face rigid with tortured emotions.

Bedlam broke out. Cheers, laughter, shouts of joy; elderly nobles went to one knee to kiss their princess's hand; younger ones brandished their dress swords overhead; ladies curtseyed until their wimples swept the floor, and rose, wet-eyed to embrace the person nearest. Lafayette jerked free of the suddenly nerveless grips on his arms to see the regent leap to his feet, his face twisted with rage.

"Imposters!" he roared. "Mummers, tricked out to resemble the dead! I myself witnessed the demise of her Highness but an hour since, and with her last breath she

173

charged me with the solemn duty of assuming the crown—"

"Let me at the conscienceless swine!" Alain roared. leaping onto the dais.

"No!" Daphne shrieked, and threw herself at him, impeding his draw as the pretender scuttled backward. "He's not a traitor, Alain. He's just temporarily lost his wits!"

"Grab him!" O'Leary yelled. "But don't hurt him," he added.

"Right!" Lord Archibald chirped as he bounded forward, chrome-plated blade bared. "We need the scoundrel in one piece for trial!"

There was a sudden disturbance behind Lafayette; he turned to see a familiar figure thrusting toward him.

"Lom!" he blurted. "Or should I say Quelius?" He reached for the little man—and froze as the sonic projector swung to cover him.

"Wait!" Lom shouted. "Don't do anything foolish! You don't know—"

"I know I want to get my hands on your skinny neck!" O'Leary yelled, and charged.

"No! You don't understand! We have to—" Lom broke off, ducked under O'Leary's clutch, whirled to face the dais.

"Queluis!" Lom roared. "Stand where you are! It's all over!"

Lafayette checked in midstride as the usurper spun to face Lom.

"You!" the regent said in a strangled tone. "But—but—but"

"That's right—me!" Lom yelled, as the man on the dais fumbled in his robes, drew out an object the size of an electric canopener, fumbled with it—

A soundless detonation sent O'Leary whirling off into lightless depths.

*The stars were rushed toward him; they struck with a ghostly impact, blasting him outward in the form of an expanding shell of thin gas. Gazing inward from all points of the compass at once, he saw all the matter in the universe, gathered at his exact center, dwindle to a single glowing point and wink out. At once he was collapsing inward, shrinking, compressing. There was a momentary sensation of searing heat and crushing weight—*

He was stumbling backward, to fetch up hard against folds of a velvet hanging against the wall. Something heavy slid down over his right eye, clanged to the floor and rolled. Below him, the man he had known as Lom looked swiftly up; his eye—as piercing as a red-hot needle—fell on O'Leary. His mouth quirked in a smile of ferocity; he raised the sonic projector—and uttered a yell as Sir Archbald brought the dull edge of his sword down on his wrist, knocking the weapon across the floor.

"I said he'll live to stand trial, you old goat!" the elderly courtier snapped. "Seize him, gentlemen! And the false regent as well!"

Eager hands grabbed Lom, who kicked and cursed in vain. And elegantly manicured hands fell on O'Leary, dragged him forward and held him, as the crowd stared up at him, wide-eyed.

"Alain," Lafayette barked. "Let go, you big oaf! It's all right now! I've got my own shape back—"

"Have done, false rogue, or I'll take pleasure in snapping your spine!"

Below, a swarthily handsome fellow in tight-fitting black with a red cummerbund stood gaping about him with an expression of total wonder.

"Zorro!" O'Leary yelled. "Tell them you're not! That you're not me anymore! I mean, that I'm not you anymore!"

"Think not to cop a plea of insanity!" Alain growled in O'Leary's ear. "There's a VIP dungeon ready and waiting for you turncoat rebel!"

"I'm not insane! I'm Lafayette O'Leary! I was somebody else, but now I'm me again, can't you understand, you numbskull? And we're not out of trouble yet—"

"How could you?" a tearful feminine voice spoke near at hand. Daphne stood there, looking up into his face. "Is it really you, Lafayette—or was that man telling the truth? That somehow you aren't really you, and—"

"Daphne—before I wasn't me—but now I am, don't you see? I'm Lafayette O'Leary, nobody else—"

"Did somebody call fer Sir Lafayette?" a deep voice boomed. Clarence appeared, making his way through the crowd with a pleased smile on his face. "Dat's me," he announced, indicating himself with a thumb. "Anybody want to make sumpin of it?"

"No, Clarence, not now!" O'Leary shouted." "Cornmeal mush!"

"Don't pay no never mind to dat bozo," Clarence exhorted the crowd. "He's a ringer. Me, I'm duh McCoy."

"Zorro!" O'Leary appealed to the Wayfarer. "I told Clarence to stick to his story until I said 'cornmeal mush.' I mean until *you* said 'cornmeal mush.' That is, I was you then, and what I meant was—"

"*I'm* duh real O'Leary!" Clarence roared.

"No, he's not!" Daphne cried. "*He* is!" She pointed at Zorro, who goggled at her in astonishment. Daphne rushed to him, threw her arms around his neck.

"I recognized you in spite of your—your disguise—as soon as you laid hands on me," she sobbed.

Zorro stared over her head; his look of amazement gave way to a delighted smile.

"You bet, keed," he said.

"Daphne!" O'Leary yelled, "get away from that degenerate! Clarence—" A loud screech cut across the room. There was a stir in the crowd, cries of outrage as a small, furious figure in a scarlet shirt, a shiny black blouse, and jungling earrings forced her way through the

176

press, followed by half a dozen olive-hued, black-haired barbarously attired Wayfarers.

"Gizelle! Luppo! What are *you* doing here?" O'Leary gasped. The girl burst through the front rank and threw herself at Zorro, who leaped from Daphne's embrace to dive for cover as his enamorata's knife whistled past his ribs.

"Peeg! Lecher! Philanderer!" Gizelle shrieked as her arms were seized and the knife clatterd away. "Wait un- teel I get my hands on you, you sneaky, feelthy worm in the weeds you!"

"Hey! Watch him!" Lafayette shouted—too late. Lom, his captor's attention distracted by the disturbance, wrenched free, ducked to catch up Gizelle's knife, darted to Daphne, now standing alone, seized her by the arm and whirled to face the crowd, holding the point of the stiletto at his captive's throat.

"Back!" he barked. "Or I slit it from ear to ear!"

Women screamed; men uttered oaths and grabbed for their sword hilts; but they fell back.

All but one man. O'Leary stared in horror as a tall, white-bearded patriarch in a glowing blue robe circled behind Lom, unseen.

The latter backed slowly, his eyes darting from face to face; he stooped, scooped up the object that the regent had been holding at the moment of O'Leary's transfer back in- to his original body.

"No!" Lafayette yelled, and plunged against the men holding him. "Don't let him—"

Lom uttered a shrill laugh. "Don't *let* me? Ha! Who can stop me?"

The tall man in blue tapped Lom on the shoulder.

"I can," he said in a tone like the tolling of a bell.

Lom whirled to goggle at the tall apparition that had ap- peared so suddenly behind him.

"Jorlemagne!" he gasped. He dropped the knife, clutched Daphne to him, thumbed a control on the button of the device in his hands—and with a sharp *whop!* of imploding air, vanished.

For the next two minutes, bedlam reigned. Lafayette made a frantic try for freedom, received a stunning blow on the skull, then hung dazedly in the grasp of the vigilantes. Confused images whirled in his brain, blended with the cacophony of a hundred voices raised in simultaneous hysteria.

"Quiet!" a thunderous tone broke through the hubbub. "Ladies and gentlemen—quiet! I must have silence in order to think!"

"Who might you be, sir?" "Where did he go?" "What's happened to Countess Daphne?" The clamor broke out again at once.

"I said quiet!" the old man roared; he made a curt gesture—and sudden, total silence fell. O'Leary could see lips moving feebly, but not a sound was audible. The crowd stood as if bemused, staring at nothing.

"Well, that's better," the old man in blue said, his voice alone audible. "Now . . ." He half closed his eyes. "Hmmm. Quelius is a tricky devil. Who'd have thought *he'd* have thought of using the Mark III in that fashion? And where would he have fled? Not the caves . . . He knows I know . . ."

*Lafayette! Help!* a silent voice rang in O'Leary's ears—or no—not in his ears. Inside his head.

*Daphne! Where are you?* He cried silently.

*It's dark! Lafayette! Lafayette. . . !*

The elder in blue was standing before him.

"Lafayette—it is *you*, isn't it? Oh, it's all right; you may speak."

"I've got to get out of here," O'Leary said. "Daphne needs me—"

"Lafayette—don't you know me?"

"Sure—I saw you in a cave, you climbed out of a coffin and tried to bite me!"

"Lafayette—I'm your ally! You knew me as Lom, an assumed name, true, but then I was hardly in a position to trust you, eh? My real name is Jorlemagne."

"*You*'re Lom? Are you out of your mind? Lom is a little shrimp under five six with a bald head and—"

"Surely you, of all people, can understand, Lafayette! Your description is of Quelius! I was caught by surprise, or he'd never have succeeded in exchanging identities with me!"

"You mean—you were Lom? And Lom was—"

"You! Simple enough, eh, now that I've explained it?"

"Wait a minute: even if you *are* Lom—or Jorlewhatsit—or whoever that was I made the jailbreak with—what makes you think I think you're any friend of mine? The way I analyzed the situation, you conned me into sneaking you into the palace so you could join forces with your sidekick, played by me—"

"But you were wrong, my boy, eh? What need to enter the palace by subterfuge if I were in fact in league with Quelius? Actually, on leaving the tower, I was trapped in a broom closet for the better part of half an hour by four palace guardsmen playing a surreptitious game of chance. When they were called away to attend a disturbance in the ballroom, I followed."

"And another thing: I've been thinking about that sudden trip to Thallathlone—wings and all. Not your doing, I suppose?"

"Oh, that. Pray forgive me, lad. At that point I was under the not unwarranted impression that *you* were Quelius' dupe. I employed a sophisticated little device which should have phased you back into what I assumed was your natural Locus—namely, Central. But naturally, since you were in fact the O'Leary ego, from Colby Corners, occupying the Zorro body—native to Artesia—the coordinates I used had the effect of switching you right out of the base-plane of the continuum. But I did keep tabs on you, and make contact as soon as you phased back in, you must concede that."

"All right—that's all gravy over the tablecloth now. What about this Quelius?"

"Ah, yes. Quelius. He planned his operation with care—but right at the beginning he made a slip. His original intention was to displace my ego into the body of a prize hog, and store my body—as well as his own—the Lom body, occupied by the mind of a pig—in a stasis tank for future use; but I was able to effect a last-second baffle and shunt my ego into his corpus, while the pig-mind occupied my unconscious body. You see?"

"No. And where was he in the meantime?"

"Oh, Quelius assumed the identity of a chap who happened along. Just as a stopgap, you understand. His real objective was to exchange identities with you."

"You mean—that wasn't really the Red Bull I met at the Ax and Dragon?"

"A large chap with bristly hair? That sounds like him. Then, after you'd been finessed into activating the Mark III, he would take over in your place, whilst you were gathered in by the local constabulary. The first part of the plan succeeded—but you slipped out of his hands somehow."

"Well—I guess I should be grateful to Luppo for that. But how did you get your own shape back?"

Jorlemagne chuckled. "I put Quelius on the spot—with your help, of course. When I pointed the sonic gun at him, he panicked and shifted back into his own body—which of course displaced me from it, to resume my own. Which in turn forced the pig personality back into its pig-body, etc, etc." Jorlemagne wagged his head. "I came to myself leaning against the royal pigsty, looking yearningly at a prize sow."

"Well—this isn't finding Quelius," O'Leary said. How did he do that disappearing act? One second they were here, and the next—phhtt!"

"The Mark III is a more versatile device than you suspect." Jorlemagne looked grave. "Now—the next problem is to deduce where he's taken her."

"That way," O'Leary said, closing his eyes and pointing. "About ten and a half miles."

"Eh? How do you know, my boy?"

"It's just a little trick I picked up from Tazlo Haz. Now let's call out the guard and—"

"A crowd of locals would merely complicate matters," Jorlemagne cut in. "You and I, lad—we'll have to tackle him alone."

"Then what are we waiting for?"

At the door the sage paused, motioned with his left forefinger; at once, the clamor in the room broke out in full force.

"Magic?" Lafayette gulped.

"Don't be silly," Jorlemagne snorted. "Microhypnotics, nothing more."

"So that's why you were always playing with your fingers—I mean Lom's fingers."

"Quelius' fingers, to be precise. He's a clever man, but he lacks the necessary digital dexterity for microhypnotics and manipulation. Pity. It would have saved a spot of bother."

"Well, we still have a spot of bother ahead. It's a hard half hour's ride, and we're wasting time."

The stable attendants stumbled over each other to accommodate them; five minutes later, mounted on stout Arabian stallions, they cantered out through the gates, galloped full tilt through the echoing street, and out along the dark road to the north.

5

The peak loomed like a giant shard of black glass into the night sky.

"High Tor, it's called," O'Leary said. "They're up there—I'm sure of it. But why there?"

"The entire formation is riddled with passages," Jorlemagne said, as the horses, winded by the run, picked

181

their way up the slope of rubble that led to the base of the mesa. "It's a natural volcanic core, left standing after the cone weathered away. Quelius spent considerable time and effort tunneling it out, under the pretext that it was to be an undercover observation station. I'll wager the Distorter gear is installed somewhere inside it. And he won't waste any time getting it in full operation, if I know Quelius—and I do."

"Well—produce one of those gadgets of yours," O'Leary urged impatiently. "I want to feel that stringy neck in my hands!"

"It's not to be quite so simple as that, my lad. My pockets are empty, I fear."

"Climbing that would be like going up the side of an apartment house," O'Leary said as he stared up at the vertical wall rising before him. He dismounted, scanned the rockface, picked a spot, hoisted himself up a few feet—and came tumbling back as his grip slipped on the smooth stone.

"A human fly couldn't go up that," he said. "We should have brought the field artillery along, and blasted a hole through it!"

"Well—we didn't," Jorlemagne said. "And since we can't walk through solid walls, we'll have to think of something else . . ."

"Hey!" O'Leary said. "You may have given me an idea. He closed his eyes, willed his thoughts back to the moment in Thallathlone when he had stood in the sealed chamber hollowed from the giant tree, abandoned there to merge—or die. He remembered the smell of the waxed, resinous wood, the sensation as he had stepped forward, pressed against and *through* the iron-hard wood . . .

*It was like wading through dense fog; a fog so thick as to drag him as he pressed forward. He felt it touch his skin, interpenetrating, swirling about his interior arrangements—and then the breaking-bubble sensation as he emerged on the far side. . . .*

He opened his eyes. He was standing in a low, stonewalled passage before a flight of rudely chipped stone steps.

"It's too bad about you, young woman," the cracked old voice was saying as Lafayette crept up the last few steps and poked his head over the threshold to the circular room, which, to judge from the ache in O'Leary's knees, occupied the topmost level of the Tor. Across the small chamber, Daphne, looking more beautiful than ever with a lock of black hair over one eye and three buttons missing from her jacket, was tugging at the handcuffs that secured her to a massive oak tree. Quelius stood looking down at her with an expression of mild reproof.

"You've caused me no end of trouble, you know—first by behaving in a most unwifely manner in refusing to espouse my regency, then by running off like a little fool, and now by saddling me with your person. Still, you'll make a useful hostage, once I've completed certain arrangements against interference."

"I never saw you before, you nasty little man," she said coolly.

"Tsk. What a pity you don't appreciate the true symmetry of the situation. As O'Leary, I paved the way for the deposition of your little featherweight princess and her lout of a consort, while at the same time destroying O'Leary's popularity with the mob—and simultaneously, established a workable police apparatus with an adequate war chest. The stage is now set for me to step in and set matters aright."

"When Lafayette catches you," Daphne said defiantly, "he'll fold you double and throw you away."

"Aha! But that's just it, my child. Lafayette will never catch me! At this moment the poor imbecile is no doubt suffering the penalty for *my* outrageous behavior!"

"Wrong!" O'Leary yelled, and launched himself at Quelius. The little old man whirled with astonishing agility, bounded to the wall, and jerked a rope dangling from above. Too late Lafayette saw the entire section of the floor before him drop like a hangman's trap. He made a wild clutch, missed, went over the edge and fell ten feet into a net that snapped shut around him like a closing fist.

7

Quelius lounged on the landing, smiling cheerfully at Lafayette, suspended in the open stairwell with his head in fetal position between his knees.

"And you were going to fold *me* double," the old fellow said good-humoredly. "Or so your bride predicted. Ah, well, we must excuse the ladies their predictable misconceptions, eh?"

"You're not going to get away with this, Quelius," Lafayette said as clearly as he could with a mouthful of kneecap. "Jorlemagne will slice you into pastrami—"

"Permit me to contradict you, Mr. O'Leary. Jorlemagne will do nothing. I'm quite immune to his digital trickery—and although he is indeed a clever chap, I happen to be in possession of the contents of his laboratory—so you see—I hold not merely the aces, but the entire deck."

"I noticed you left the ballroom in something of a hurry," O'Leary countered. "I suppose being in your burrow makes you feel brave. But I got inside without much trouble, you notice."

"So you did," Quelius nodded imperturbably. "My instruments indicate that you empoyed a rather interesting molecular polarization technique to pull off the trick. I invite you to use the same method to extricate yourself from your present situation." He crackled merrily. "You've been a sore trial to me, O'Leary. Bad stroke of luck, encountering Hymie the Ferocious, I believe he called himself, when I stepped outside the tavern that night. My, I'll warrant the red-headed ruffian whose shape I was using

184

had skinned knuckles when he came to himself. But for that interruption you'd have been safely tucked away in the palace brig, ready to assist me in my impersonation. But then, all's well that ends well."

"Why go to so much trouble to strand yourself in a backward Locus like Artesia?" Lafayette inquired.

"Just making conversation, O'Leary? But I may as well oblige you; the Distorter won't be up to full charge for another half hour or so. Why Artesia, you ask? Well, I find it ideally suited to my purposes. Too backward to possess adequate techniques of self-defense, but sufficiently advanced to offer the industrial base I require to construct the masterwork of my career."

"So what? Nobody here will be able to appreciate it—and you're cutting off all contact with Central, so no one there will ever know."

"Correction," Quelius beamed. He rubbed his hands together with a sound like sand blocks in a kindergarten orchestra. "I estimate it will require no more than a year to assemble a high-capacity Distorter capable of acting effectively, against the Probability gradient. My, won't the pompous officials of Central—those self-appointed monitors of continuum morality—be surprised when they discover that it's their own bureaucratic beehive that's cut off from all outside contact? And then, O'Leary—then I can set about rearranging matters in a manner more to my liking!"

"Quelius—you're nuts—did you know that?"

"Of course. That's quite all right. Better embarked on an exciting insanity than moldering away in dull normality. One thing you can't deny: we psychotics lead interesting lives." Quelius dropped his bantering tone. "Now," he said briskly, "it's time to make disposition of you, Mr. O'Leary, and see to my equipment. Now, I could merely cut the rope and allow you to continue your interrupted descent—or I might lower you to a point six feet above the cellar floor and build a small fire to keep the chill off your bones. Any preference, Mr. O'Leary?"

"Sure. I'd prefer to die of old age."

"To be sure, so would we all—all but myself, of course. I'll have available to me an endless series of fresh young vessels to contain the vital essence of my personality. Possibly I'll begin with Mrs. O'Leary, eh? It might be quite a lark to be a female—until I tired of the game; but this isn't solving the problem of your brief future. Hmm. I may have an idea—if you'll excuse me a moment. Now don't go 'way." Quelius cackled and hurried off.

The stoutly woven net, of quarter-inch hemp, rotated slowly, affording O'Leary an ever-changing aspect of damp stone walls. Hanging head-down as he was, he had an equally clear view of the floor a hundred feet below. He imagined how it would feel when the knife blade began sawing through the rope. First one strand would break, and the net would drop a few inches; then another—and another—and at last the final popping sound and the downward plunge—

"That kind of thinking won't help any, O'Leary," he told himself sternly. "Maybe Jorlemagne has a trick or two up his sleeve. Maybe a regiment of Royal Cavalry are riding to the rescue right now; maybe Daphne will free the cuffs and bean the old devil when he pokes his head in the room . . ."

"Maybe you'd like to take part in an experiment?" Quelius called as he came pattering back down the stairs. "Actually, it's wasteful to merely cast aside a valuable experimental animal—and as it happens, I have a new modification on one of Jorlemagne's little trinkets I'd like to put to trial. It will take a few moments to set things up, but please be patient."

By rolling his eyes, Lafayette could see the renegade Commissioner setting out an armload of equipment on the landing. There was a tripod, a spherical, green-painted object the size of a softball, wires, pipes, a heavy black box.

"Jorlemagne intended the device as an aide to medical examination," Quelius confided as he worked. "Gives the surgeons a superb view of one's insides, eh? It required only a slight shifting about of components to improve it, however. My version simply turns the subject inside out, with no nonsense. Liver and lights right there for handy inspection. Of course, there's a bit of difficulty when it comes to getting you put back in the original order afterward, but after all, we can't expect the pilot model to be without bugs, eh?"

Lafayette closed his eyes. No point in spending his last moments listening to the raving of a madman when he could be remembering pleasant scenes of the past for the last time. He pictured Daphne's smiling face . . . but the vision of her chained to a chair rose to blot out the image. He thought of Adoranne and Alain—and pictured them humbled before Quelius as he lolled on his stolen throne flanked by his secret police. Jorlemagne's towering figure was there—shaking his head futilely. Luppo rose up; Gizelle looked at him tearfully. Belarius stared at him accusingly; Agent Raunchini shook a fist at him, mouthing reproaches. The lean visage of Wizner Hiz was there, alight with triumph as he led his choral group in song . . .

Lafayette opened his eyes. Quelius was busily stringing wires.

"Won't be a moment, O'Leary. Don't be impatient," he called.

Lafayette cleared his throat, and started to sing:

*Out of the world*
*        Away and beyond*
*Back through the veil*
*        Quelius begone . . .*

"What's this?" The oldster looked around in surprise. "Vocal renditions in the face of eternity? A notable display of pluck. Pity your bride will never know. I intend to tell her that you kicked and screamed, offered to trade her for your life, volunteered to cut her ears off and all that sort of thing. Most amusing to watch her attempting to keep a stiff upper lip."

187

*Afloat on a sea*
  *Wider than night*
*Deeper and deeper*
  *Sinking from sight*

"Catchy tune," Quelius said. "Interesting rhythm. Seems to be a variation on the natural reality harmonic. Curious. Where did you learn it?"

*Back where you came from,*
  *Stealer of thrones*
*Back to the depths*
  *Far under the stones . . .*

"You're annoying me, O'Leary," Quelius snapped. He had stopped work to glare at his captive. "Stop that caterwauling at once!"

*Out of the world,*
  *Far from the sun*
*Begone from Artesia*
  *Forever begone!*

"Stop it at once, do you hear?" Quelius shrieked, covering his ears. "You're making me dizzy!" Suddenly he snatched up a knife from the heap of tools at his feet, leaned far out and slashed at the rope supporting the net.

*Borne on the wings*
  *Of the magic song*
*From Fair Artesia*
  *Forever begone!"*

There was a sharp *pop!* The rasping of the knife against the rope ceased abruptly. In the sudden silence, O'Leary thought he heard a faint, faraway cry, that trailed off into silence. . . .

Footsteps rasped on the stone steps. O'Leary pried an eye open, saw Jorlemagne leaning out to pull the net in to the landing.

". . . found the entry . . . few minutes to discover trick . . . Quelius . . . where is he—" the scientist's voice boomed and faded.

"Daphne—upstairs . . ." Lafayette managed; and then the darkness folded in like a black comforter.


# 8


Lafayette awoke lying on his back in a narrow white bed. An anxious-looking old fellow whom he recognized as the royal physician was hovering over him.

"Ah, awake at last, are we, sir? Now, just rest quietly—"

"Where's Daphne?" O'Leary sat up, threw off the covers.

"Sir Lafayette! I must insist! You've been unconscious for two days—"

"Nonsense! I've never felt better. Where is she?"

"Why—ah—as to that—Countess Daphne is in her apartments—in seclusion. She, er, doesn't wish to be disturbed—"

"Don't be silly, I don't want to disturb her." Lafayette leaped up, staggering only slightly, and grabbed up a robe from the chair beside the bed.

"But, Sir Lafayette, you can't—"

"Just watch me!"

"Two minutes later, O'Leary rapped on Daphne's door. "It's me, Lafayette!" he called. "Open up, Daphne!"

"Go away," came a muffled reply.

"Lafayette—what seems to be the trouble?" Jorlemagne called, arriving at a trot. "Dr. Ginsbag told me you'd leaped up and dashed off in a frenzy!"

"What's the matter with Daphne? She won't open the door!"

The old gentleman spread his hands. "Poor child, she's been through so much. I suggest you give her a few weeks to recover from the shock—"

"A few weeks! Are you out of your beanie? I want to see her *now!*" He pounded on the door again. "Daphne! Open this door!"

"Go away, you imposter!"

"Imposter—" Lafayette whirled to the startled sentries flanking the door. "All right, boys—break it down!"

As they hesitated, shuffling their feet and exhanging anxious glances, the door was flung open. Daphne stood there, dabbing at tear-reddened eyes. She jumped back as Lafayette reached for her.

"Leave me alone, you . . . you makeup artist," she wailed. "I knew you weren't really Lafayette the minute you threw the soup tureen at the Second cook!"

"Daphne—that was all a mistake! I wasn't really me then, but I am now!"

"No, you're not; you're a stranger! And Lafayette is a horrid man with a gold ring in his ear and the whitest teeth, and the most immense black eyes, and . . ."

"That's Zorro, the crook!" O'Leary yelled. "I was him for a while, while Quelius was me, but now I'm me again, and so is he!"

"I recognized him when he kissed me—"

"Almost kissed you," Lafayette corrected. "I stopped in time, remember?"

"I mean the next time. And then . . . and then he went away with that little dark-eyed creature with the knife—and he . . . he stole my gold bracelet before he left!"

"Daphne! What's been going on here? Don't tell me! Zorro is Zorro—and I'm me! Lafayette! Look at me! Don't you know me, Daphne?"

"My dear Countess," Jorlemagne started, "I assure you—"

"Stay out of this!" O'Leary yelled. "Daphne! Remember the fountain in the gardens where we used to sit and feed the goldfish? Remember the time you dropped the chamber pot on Alain's head? Remember the dress—the rose-colored silk one? Remember the time you saved me when I was falling off the roof?"

"If . . . if you're actually Lafayette," Daphne said, facing him "when is my mother's birthday?"

"Your mother's birthday? Ah . . . let's see . . . uh . . . in October?"

"Wrong! What night are we supposed to play bridge with the duchess?"

"Er . . . Wednesday?"

"Wrong! When is our anniversary?"

"I know that one," Lafayette cried in relief. "The third of next month!"

"He's an imposter," Daphne wailed. "Lafayette never remembered our anniversary!" She turned and fled into the room, threw herself facedown on the bed, weeping. Lafayette hurried after her.

"Don't touch me!" she cried as he bent over her.

"Oh, this is fine," O'Leary groaned. "Just perfect! Why did I have to do such a convincing job of selling you on my identity when I was Zorro?"

"It wasn't so much what he said," Daphne wept, "it was the way he made love that convinced me . . . and now he's gone . . ."

"Daphne! I keep telling you—you—what?" O'Leary's voice rose to a squeak. "Give me air!" he yelped, and plunged through the doors to the balcony—

And fell twenty feet into a rhododendron bush.

Daphne was sitting on the ground, cradling his head in her lap.

"Lafayette—is it really you—"

"I . . . I've been telling you . . ."

"But it has to be. The false Lafayette was the one who ordered the balcony removed, when he tried to lock me in our apartments. *He* would have known it wasn't there. And besides—nobody but my very own Lafayette falls down quite the way you do!"

"Daphne," O'Leary murmured, and drew her down to him. . . .

"I just happened to think," Daphne said later. "If you were Zorro—just what was your relationship with that little brunette baggage named Gizelle?"

"*I* was wondering what *your* sleeping arrangements were—up until that four-flusher showed his true colors—"

"But then," Daphne went on as if he hadn't spoken, "I decided there are some questions best left unasked."